New Blood

The Billionaires' Club: Book 8

AE Moran

The Invisible Publishing Company

The Billionaires' Club Series

Contents

Chapter 1: Kevin

I come out of the office in The Billionaires' Club and head for the electrical panel to check this month's meter reading. "Don't you ever stop working?" Rory Kahn grabs me and pulls me into a group with Diego Espinosa, Giovanni Nowaczyk, and Jackson Metcalf.

"You should listen to Diego's new proposal, Kevin," Jackson tells me. "You would probably be interested in a piece of that action."

Diego points at me. "Yes, Kevin. I would be interested in doing business with you."

I glance around the group. "Can't we discuss this another time? I'm in the middle of something."

"Is it something related to your business?" Giovanni asks. "Let me guess. It's something for the club."

"What's wrong with that?" I ask. "I am one of the officers in this club the last time I checked."

"You're the membership officer," Jackson reminds me. "*I'm* the finance officer the last time I checked."

I shove this month's power bill into his hands. "You can double-check the meter reading, then. The power company got it wrong again."

He frowns at the bill and then his expression clears. He stuffs the bill into his inner jacket pocket. "All right. I'll take care of it."

Now it's my turn to frown. "*When* will you take care of it?"

"That's my business. You're here to enjoy yourself, not to do another man's job for him."

I groan and roll my eyes at the other guys. They laugh at me.

"This contract of mine, Kevin," Diego interrupts.

"Is it another military contract?" I ask.

"Is that a problem for you?"

"That depends on what you're contracting."

"I'm contracting medical equipment," he replies. "You can't have a problem with that, can you?"

"I don't deal in medical equipment," I tell him. "I do personnel."

"That's what I want to talk to you about. I want to talk to you about supplying my military contracts with the personnel necessary to operate the medical equipment I provide. What do you think of that?"

I cock my head to study him. "That sounds interesting. I might be interested to hear more."

He smiles at me across the circle. He isn't the youngest man in the room, but he isn't the oldest, either. He's in his late thirties at the oldest.

He *is* the only member of the club who's from another country. He's Spanish, but he's been in the US for decades. He hasn't lost his accent in all those years. He still sounds like he just got off the plane.

We've all done business with him, including me. That's how I know so much about him. What I know always makes me ask a lot of questions before I go into business with him again.

He deals almost exclusively in government and military contracts. Some of them are harmless and ordinary. This medical equipment contract sounds like it might be one of those.

Then again, it might not be. Some people say he flies certain things under the radar with a contract that only appears harmless and ordinary on the surface while underneath hiding something that is neither harmless nor ordinary.

He's never done anything like that with me and I don't know of anyone who says he does it, but there's a first time for everything. I just keep my eye on him when I do business with him.

Maybe it's the government who flies these things under Diego's radar the same way the government flies them under everyone else's. Maybe he really doesn't know anything about it.

I've known the guy for years. He doesn't approve of underhanded tactics, not even from the government—especially not from the US government. He's one of the most patriotic sticklers for law and order that I know and he isn't even originally from this country.

I would have to investigate any business deal we did together. He's never caught me in a deal I later regretted or came to disapprove of, but I know other people who suspect him of it. Some of those people are right here in this room.

He pulls out his phone and starts tapping on it. "I'll send you the information, Kevin. You can take a look and....."

"Who is that?" Rory murmurs from my right.

I glance at him and see him staring past my shoulder at something behind me. I turn the other way and find myself looking at a tall woman with impeccable makeup and tiny round hoop earrings peeking out from under her perfectly styled short blonde hair.

She wears a casual, cropped denim blazer, a white pencil skirt around her tight, shapely figure, and tall ankle boots that make her look even taller than she Is.

She carries an alligator-skin purse under one arm and looks around the club in all directions. She's the only woman in here.

I say, "I'll handle this," to the guys near me and walk over to her. "Can I help you, Ma'am? This is a private club."

"I....uh....." She looks everywhere but at me. "I......I might have the wrong place. I was told this was where The Billionaires' Club meets."

"It is, but this club is members only." I frown at her. "Can I ask who told you that? That information isn't public knowledge."

She attacks her purse and fumbles to pull out a tiny scrap of paper. "I met a woman downtown yesterday. She told me about this place and she said I should come by here and.....I have her name here....she gave it to me and she gave me the address....she said she was a lawyer.....Oh, here it is. Her name is Piper Legrange." She looks straight up into my eyes. "Do you know her?"

I can't stop frowning at her. "Piper told you to come here? Why? Piper is one of the members' wives. She knows the club is private."

"I met her at a networking function. She said I should come because I just passed the billion-dollar net worth mark.....and I don't know anyone else in town. She said I should come...." She glances around again. "But maybe I made a mistake. I didn't realize I would be the only woman here."

"You're the only woman here right now, but you wouldn't be the only female member of the club. We do have other female billionaires in the club." I hold out my hand. "I'm Kevin Drake. I'm the club membership officer, so if you did apply to join, I would be the one handling your application."

Her head shoots up and she bursts into a smile when she shakes my hand. "It's nice to meet you! I'm Paige Novak. Thank you so much! I was really worried when I walked in and saw only men here."

"Piper should have told you." I wave behind me. "Do you want me to introduce you to some of the guys?"

"I...um....." She glances past me and winces. "I'm not sure if I'm ready for that. Do you mind if we just talk one-on-one? My company just took off recently. All this billionaire stuff is still new to me and... .well...intimidating."

"I understand completely. I hear that a lot from people whose companies started from nothing and then skyrocketed. Hardly anyone here came into the club from old money."

Her eyes widen. "Did that happen to you? Did you have to fight your way in?"

I laugh. "Me? No, my family has old money, but I left home right after high school and made my own way. I wanted to be able to call my success my own and not have people telling me all the time that they gave me a leg up."

Her eyes twinkle. She has clear blue eyes that express so much depth and unguarded emotion. "Good for you. What's your business?"

"I'm in personnel. I'm a people broker. I match up all kinds of businesses with the right people for whatever they need. I've done business with almost everyone in the club—because everybody needs people." I frown at her. "Are you sure you don't want me to introduce you? I would hate to think you came all the way over here to talk to one person."

She laughs. She has a musical, infectious laugh that makes me instantly like her. "If I talked to one person, that's a step up from none—which is how many I knew before I came in here. I just moved to town and I don't know anyone—except my husband, of course. He moved up here with me."

"Where did you move from?"

"North Carolina." She grimaces at the New York skyline outside the windows. "My father used to talk about New York City like it was on the moon. I never thought I'd set foot in this town, let alone move here."

"So what brought you? What's your business?"

"I moved here because my business got too big for North Carolina. I developed a line of state-of-the-art medical equipment that I'm supplying to the government, military, and some of the biggest medical provider companies in the country." She passes her hand across her eyes. "I'm still trying to believe it's really happening."

"Hold up a second. Are you doing business with Diego Espinosa?"

"Yes!" She practically jumps in the air. "How did you guess? Do you know him? Could you introduce me? I've been communicating with him via email and I'm really anxious to meet him. He wants to buy a bunch of my equipment and I'm really curious about the person on the other end."

"He's right over there." I jerk my thumb over my shoulder. "He's a good friend of mine. In fact, he was just asking me if I would supply the personnel to run the equipment."

Her jaw drops. "No way! You mean....I'm actually in the same room with him right now?! I don't believe it!"

"Come on over. Then you can say you actually talked to two people instead of just one."

I turn away to lead her back to the group. She lunges for me, holds onto my arm, and giggles like a little kid. "This is so thrilling!" she murmurs. "I can't believe I'm actually meeting billionaires!"

I have to laugh. This is the first time a potential applicant has acted so excited about meeting us.

I lead her over to the group and introduce her to everyone, including Diego. They talk at length and he explains to her again that he wants me to supply the personnel to run the equipment.

"You should also talk to Dante Helme," Jackson tells her. "He runs a whole care facility empire. He would probably be interested in your equipment, too."

"That sounds great!" She beams at everyone and she turns to me. "It's like I told you. The equipment is state-of-the-art and, in some cases, still in the prototype stages. We would need people to go through special training to be able to run the equipment."

"My company can handle that, too," I tell her. "We can set up the training programs with your people running them and offering instruction. Then my organization will provide the trained personnel to anyone you supply to. We can link the two contracts so only people trained under our program are qualified for positions requiring them to run the equipment."

"Yes, Kevin!" Diego claps his hands. "That is exactly what I was thinking!"

Paige bursts into one of her dazzling, blinding grins at me. "That sounds perfect. How about I send you all the information and we can communicate about it?"

"Great." I take out my phone. "Give me your number and your email address and I'll give you mine. Then you can contact me about applying for club membership, too."

She blushes and giggles again. "I'm going to be a member of the club! Yay!"

A bunch of people laugh at her attitude. Her enthusiasm is impossible to resist. Everyone smiles at her.

"We're having a club gala next week, too," I tell her. "I can arrange for you to get an invitation even if you aren't a member yet. We can invite you as a guest and you could bring your husband and meet everyone in a casual social setting. Then you can warm up to people, get reacquainted with people you already know, and see if you really like it enough to join."

"That sounds awesome! I would love that."

"You can call any of us if you need help settling into town," Jackson adds. "Everyone wants to help new members get oriented and feeling comfortable with the rest of us."

She beams at him. "That is so generous of you. Thank you so much."

She and I exchange details and she waves her phone at everyone. "Thank you all so much for being so welcoming. I was scared out of my pants to come in here and meet a bunch of strangers. This is going to be great. I'll see you all around."

They all wave and say, "Bye, Paige!" She leaves.

"She was delightful," Giovanni remarks. "She's a breath of fresh air—exactly what the club needs."

"She was really sweet," Jackson agrees and he turns to me. "She seemed taken with you."

"She was just glad to meet someone who welcomed her."

"She's gorgeous," Diego adds. "Her husband is a lucky man whoever he is."

Chapter 2: Paige

I step out onto the sidewalk outside The Billionaires' Club and breathe a sigh of relief. They were all so sweet and kind and welcoming. I can't believe I worked myself up into such a state of anxiety over meeting them.

They're all just normal people—except that they're all much nicer and more understanding. Kevin is an absolute sweetheart.

He has bright green eyes, curly auburn hair, and an extremely soft, friendly, warm manner. I really got lucky meeting him first. Jackson seems like a really nice person, too. They all do.

I take another shaky breath. I got over that hurdle. Everything else should be easy—and I got all these new business contacts, too. I'm thrilled with Kevin's suggestion that we partner to train the personnel to run my equipment. I was really worried about that.

I set off walking down the sidewalk. I'm floating on air. Moving to New York is turning out to be so much better than I expected.

I turn a corner, approach a car parked at the curb, and get in on the passenger side. My husband Trent sits in the driver's seat.

"You aren't going to believe it!" I exclaim. "I was so nervous going in, but they were all so nice and I got talking to Kevin Drake, the membership officer, and he suggested we do a deal to supply the personnel to run my equipment! And Diego Espinosa was there! He's a member of the club! Can you believe it?! Phew! That was awesome! I can't believe I actually went in there—and Kevin invited me to go to the club gala next week!"

Trent turns around in his seat and glares at me. "Is that so?"

I see the look in his eyes. "He said I could come with you—not that I would go with him! He said he could invite us as guests even if I'm not a member of the club yet."

He sneers at me. "Was there a single woman in there just now? Tell the truth."

"No, but he said the other female members...."

"You can't ever go back," he snaps. "Do you hear me? This whole club thing—it's over. You're not going to become a member and you sure as hell aren't going to any gala with some other guy named Kevin."

I frown at him and then try to wave that away. "I just told you I would go with you! He's the one who would invite us—both of us—as guests! See? I wouldn't go with him! He's just a really nice person. He came over to talk to me because he didn't know why I was there and the club is supposed to be private."

"I don't give a damn what he said. You aren't joining any club, especially not a club full of men."

"I'm not the only female billionaire in the club!" I counter. "I mean...I wouldn't be if I joined. They just weren't there today—right this minute. They're probably all working."

"But these dudes all have time to stand around hitting on any woman who walks through the door?"

"They didn't hit on me, Trent. Not one single person in there hit on me—and now I got all these great business contacts."

He turns away and starts the car. "I knew moving to New York was a bad idea. We never should have left North Carolina."

I wilt in my seat and all my enthusiasm goes cold at those words. "We had to move. The company couldn't grow any more in North Carolina."

"You and that company! All you care about is the company! You should have given it up a long time ago. Then we wouldn't be in this mess."

I gulp. "What mess is that?"

"We should just move back home right now before the situation gets any worse."

"I can't move back home now. I'm already in negotiations with Diego Espinosa. We're slated to meet later this week to iron out the details of a contract that could put SigmaTech on the map."

He snorts, puts the car into gear, and sets off driving down the street. "You are not going back to that club—not ever. Do you understand me? You are not going around rubbing elbows with a bunch of men I've never met. Stay away from them. Stay away from the club and stay away from this Kevin character. He sounds like a sleaze."

He drives off down the street and turns a few corners. I haven't learned my way around New York well enough to understand exactly where he's going or where anything is in relation to anything else.

I'm too torn and confused about this to even think about where he's going or where anything is.

I can't ignore these contacts. They offer too many opportunities for my company to grow. I didn't work this hard to make SigmaTech a success to let it all slip away now when we're finally getting the traction we need.

So how am I going to deal with Trent's attitude? He seems bent on destroying SigmaTech just when it's starting to take off and succeed. He never had a problem with my work while we lived in North Carolina.

He also had no problem with us moving to New York—not until we actually got here. This is the first time he's come right out and said point blank that he wants to leave and move back home. I didn't realize he'd gone that far in his hostility to this place.

He seems especially hostile toward Kevin for some reason. I can't imagine why since Trent has never met Kevin or any of the other billionaires.

That seems to be the problem right there. All the men at the club are billionaires and I'm a billionaire. Trent isn't one.

He was the one who insisted that we keep our money separate both while we were dating and after we got married. He made it seem at the time that he didn't want money issues to interfere with our relationship. He didn't want money to be a part of that.

Now I see it differently. He might have wanted to protect himself from me trying to get to *his* money. Now he sees me becoming a billionaire while he gets left behind.

Maybe he wants to share my money after all. Maybe he's starting to realize that he could be a billionaire now if he had agreed to share our money from the beginning—or maybe he wouldn't want to become a billionaire on my success.

Either way, he has a massive problem with me being a billionaire. He has a massive problem with everything related to SigmaTech's success. I don't see how this can work without me giving up one or the other. Something has to give.

Chapter 3: Paige

Trent drops me off in front of the new SigmaTech office building. I think it might be on Seventh Avenue, but I'm still not quite sure. It's somewhere in midtown Manhattan.

It's going to take me a while to figure out all the different boroughs and how they work in relation to each other. Forget about me driving anywhere. No one would ever see me again.

I ride the elevator up to my fancy new office on the thirtieth floor. All the company executive officers work up here. My office is at the far end of the building with two corner windows looking north toward Central Park.

I love the view, but sometimes it intimidates me so much that I can't look at it. I don't want to think about the fact that I'm in New York City.

I can pretend as long as I keep my back turned to the window that I'm still in North Carolina and working in my old office there. That's all I have to do. I just have to keep running the company the way I did before we moved.

I field a bunch of phone calls from the production department and then I get into an email discussion with Diego about our upcoming contract negotiations. We send the specs back and forth and then he cc's a few other people into our conversation.

One of them is Montgomery Sinclair, whom Diego informs me is one of his business partners, and Emerson Sinclair, Montgomery Sinclair's son, whom Diego informs me is also Montgomery Sinclair's business partner.

Diego also cc's in two US Army generals who are in charge of negotiations between Diego's supply company and the Pentagon.

The US military wants to include some slight modifications to the equipment to make the pieces more mobile. The military wants to deploy our machines in mobile hospitals, on Navy vessels, and other places the equipment might need to be moved around.

Diego also cc's Kevin into the conversation. The rest of us keep firing emails back and forth for a long time before Kevin gets involved. He sends me a message about the training programs we need to implement to train personnel.

He and I start getting into a back-and-forth about that before he suggests that we separate this conversation from the others. It isn't really relevant to what I'm discussing with them.

Then he and I go back and forth just between ourselves about the training program. I send him everything we have so far and he gets super enthusiastic about this. He says he can accommodate this with no problem.

He suggests we meet in person to finalize the deal. Then his company, People, Inc., can hammer out a separate contract with SigmaTech that will allow us to contract jointly with the other parties involved.

His enthusiasm becomes infectious and I get super excited about this, too. This is gonna be great.

I get back on the line with Diego and the others to inform them that People, Inc. and SigmaTech will be negotiating jointly to provide trained personnel to operate the equipment.

The generals come back and explain that they'll obviously want to send their own people through Kevin's training program. I let Kevin know.

Of course he doesn't have a problem with that. We're talking about multiple multi-billion-dollar government contracts. This could be the deal of a lifetime for all of us.

Kevin and I make an appointment to meet in person later in the week. We set up the time and day—and then he sends me all the information about applying to become a member of The Billionaires' Club.

He also sends a guest invitation for two to the next club gala. It's a formal affair requiring the attendees to dress formally. The venue is the ballroom of one of the biggest, ritziest hotels in town. Wow. This is huge.

I sit in my chair staring at the screen. I really, super want to go to this gala and meet all the other billionaires—especially the other female billionaires.

Piper Legrange told me in our brief meeting that the billionaires' wives are all good friends, that they're involved in each other's lives, and they all go out of their way to support each other and their spouses.

I want to meet them all. I want to talk to them about everything. I want to find out if any of them ever had to deal with a hostile spouse like Trent.

My heart drops into my stomach when I read both the invitation to the gala and the information about applying to the club. Trent will never let me apply or go to the gala.

Kevin informs me that the club is private, that only billionaire members are allowed inside, and that the club is supposed to be a place for the billionaires to socialize with others in their own income bracket without fear of judgment from anyone else.

That description definitely fits Trent. Kevin sends me pre-prepared PDFs of club documents that have obviously been written for any random prospective applicant to read. He didn't write that specifically meaning Trent, but the shoe definitely fits.

I sigh and navigate away from the documents and the invitation. I thank Kevin for the information and don't mention them again in our next couple of exchanges. I keep our conversation business-related.

Maybe Trent will come around and change his mind. I can only hope.

I've only been in New York for a few days. Everything is brand new. I don't need to join The Billionaires' Club right this minute. I'm already doing business with two of them.

I'm going to be living in New York for a long time if SigmaTech keeps booming the way it has been. I'll have all the time in the world to talk Trent into going along with this and to get to know all the club members and their wives and husbands.

I really need this club. I realize that now. I didn't want to admit it to myself, but I had been drifting away from my old friends and contacts in North Carolina. I didn't change, but they did. They let my money interfere in our relationships.

They acted like I was the one who changed when I was the same person I had always been. They pulled away. They acted like I was insulting them when I tried to keep associating with them in the old way.

Maybe that's what's happening between me and Trent. I almost dread going home for the day, but I have to. I have to face him and deal with him one way or the other.

He wants me to call him so he can come and pick me up from work. He has this idea that he's going to chauffeur me around town and take me everywhere I go—probably so I don't interact with anyone but him.

I should call him now, but I want to start getting used to living in this city. I decide to take a risk and catch a cab home.

We're moving into a big penthouse apartment on the upper floor of a high-rise on the other side of midtown.

The cab driver is a really nice Sikh man who talks to me the whole way there. He tells me where everything is, where his family lives, where his relatives operate businesses, and he encourages me to go patronize them if I want to. He tells me he'll hook me up with discounts for all of them.

I thank him, give him a huge tip, and hustle inside the building to ride the elevator up to the penthouse. I find Trent carrying boxes into the apartment, unpacking them, and rearranging the furniture that came with the place.

The penthouse is a big, split-level, modern luxury apartment with three living spaces on separate levels and a big rooftop terrace extending over a different part of the building.

The bedrooms and additional bathrooms are on an upstairs section behind the living area. That leaves the big windows free so we can enjoy the view.

The furniture is all modern, minimalistic, and extremely chic. I absolutely love the apartment, the ultra-modern kitchen, immaculate bathrooms, and the sweeping view.

Trent makes it hard to love this apartment by glaring at me the minute I walk through the door. I try to keep it positive by smiling at him and kissing him. "Hi, sweetie!" I greet him.

"I told you I wanted to drive you to and from work," he snaps. "I don't know what you're doing running around out there."

"I didn't want to interrupt you." I pick up one of the boxes and bring it inside. "I guess the movers couldn't get into the apartment without a key."

He makes a face at the apartment and actually curls his lip at the windows and the view. "This place is too big. We should have gotten something smaller."

I lose my patience with him. It's been wearing thin these last few days, but his attitude toward the club is really starting to get to me. Who am I supposed to get support from if not the other billionaires? I sure as hell am not getting it from him.

"You were the one who always used to complain about us not having enough money to do fun things and go on nice vacations," I counter. "You can't complain about it now when we finally do have the money to do all those things."

"Well, we haven't done any fun things or gone on any nice vacations, have we?" he fires back. "You're always working on that company of yours."

"Well, where am I supposed to get the money to do those things if I don't work? The money has to come from somewhere. Besides, we're in New York now. We can do all the fun things you want to do." I glide over to him, slip my arm around his waist, and ease in to murmur in his ear. "We could go on a romantic date, have dinner in a fancy restaurant, and go out to see a show on Broadway."

He shrugs me off and stops short of actually throwing his elbow at me to push me away. "I'm sure you can find just about any guy in town to do all those things with you. I'm busy here."

"What is your problem?" I counter. "This is the whole reason I started this company in the first place. Remember? We had a decent lifestyle in North Carolina, but you said it wasn't enough and we needed more. You said we needed a nicer house, a nicer car, and more sophisticated friends. That's why I started SigmaTech—because you wanted us to be better than everyone we grew up with. Now we're here. We have all the things you said you wanted and all you do is bitch and complain about everything, including the fact that I have to work to support us. Pull your head out of your ass."

He spins around to yell at me. "I'm not going to be happy about you spending all your time with strangers and making eyes at every guy you do business with. You're the one leaving me in the dust and you're too blind to even see that. You would quit that stupid company if you really cared about me."

"I am not going to quit the company, Trent!" I fire back. "You can put that out of your head right now. I sank my heart and soul into this company—not to mention blood, sweat, tears, and years of my life. This company is just getting big enough that we might actually be able to do some good in the world. I'm not going to walk away from that just because you're acting like a spoiled brat. I've given you everything you've ever wanted and I have never looked at another guy since the day we met. I'm losing massive amounts of respect for you that you're so threatened by my success when you aren't even trying to do anything remotely productive. You don't even have a job and you complain about me working to support you. We have this nice penthouse because of me. Remember? You're trying to drag me down and I'm done with it."

He doesn't even hear the last part. He shifts his weight to his other foot and points in my face. "Just hear this. If you get involved with any man in business—especially anyone from The Billionaires' Club—I want to be present in the room to make sure there's nothing going on. I want to be there so none of these jackasses making any moves on y ou."

"That's ridiculous. We'll be talking business—nothing else."

He raises both hands and turns away. "Those are my terms. Take them or leave them. I want to be present anytime you meet any other man in any business capacity whatsoever. I don't trust these guys as far as I can throw them."

"That's just nuts, Trent. Hundreds of men already work for Sig-maTech."

"Them, too," he counters. "I don't want you in the same room with them—not unless I'm there."

I stare at him in blank disbelief. He can't be serious—but he is. He's completely off his rocker if he actually expects this to work.

I get a brief mental flash of what it would look like if I brought Trent to a business negotiation with Diego, his business partners, and two generals from the Pentagon.

That's what we're talking about here. I would be bringing my broke, deadbeat, unemployed husband to a billion-dollar military contract negotiation so he can keep tabs on me. It would be laughable if it wasn't so disastrously, catastrophically, outrageously unaccept-able.

This can only end badly, but he won't change his mind. He's so fixated on this idea that he won't let it go.

Now I'm the one who raises my hands in surrender. "Fine. I'll inform them if that's the way you want it."

He mutters, "You better," and goes back to what he was doing.

Chapter 4: Kevin

I flag the waiter and ask him for the check before I turn back to the woman in front of me. "Are you sure you don't want me to give you a ride across town?" I ask. "I really don't like letting you go off alone like this."

She wipes a tissue across her cheeks. "I need to take a walk outside by myself for a while. I need to think about things and make a decision about how I'm going to proceed. I have a lot on my mind lately."

I extend my hand across the table and clasp hers. I lean forward and lower my voice to a murmur. "Listen to me. I want you to call me if you need anything—anything at all. Understand? Don't get all proud and self-reliant and all that. There is nothing wrong with you asking for help—not now or anytime in the future. I mean it. I want to know the minute you feel like going back to work. There's no reason for you to sit around your apartment feeling hopeless about everything."

She nods fast and pinches her lips trying to control herself, but she can't stop the tears from running down her cheeks. "Thank you, Kevin!" she howls. "I don't know what I would do without your support."

The waiter brings the check just then. I hand him my credit card and stand up. "Come on. Let's get out of here."

I help her out of the booth, pull her into a hug, and kiss her on top of the head. She holds onto me extra tight and sobs into my jacket.

"Everything is going to be all right," I murmur. "You're going to bounce back from this. I know you are—but don't forget to lean on your friends. You have my number."

"Thank you!" she moans.

I push her back and wait for her to wipe her face again. The waiter comes back with my card and the receipt. I sign it, scribble down what I want him to tip himself, and he thanks me before he leaves.

I take the woman's hand and lead her outside where I hug her again. "Call me," I tell her again. "Seriously. I'll be extremely upset if you don't."

"Okay," she chokes. "Thank you."

I nudge her shoulder and push her away. "Go on, then. Enjoy your walk. I'll see you next week."

She nods again and walks off. I take that moment to pull out my phone and check my messages. I'm just following up with some of my people who will be implementing the SigmaTech training. This deal is turning out to be a goldmine for everyone involved.

I'm thinking about something completely different when someone touches my elbow. "Kevin?"

I look up and find Paige standing next to me. "Hi!" I greet her.

She bursts into one of those electric grins of hers. "Hi. Can I take it to mean from your reaction that you remember who I am?"

"How could I forget? How you doing? Are you okay? Are you lost?"

She breaks out in that infectious laugh of hers. "No, I'm not lost. I was having a business lunch with someone and I saw you in there....." She waves toward the café where I just had my meeting. "I was actually waiting for you to come out. I wasn't trying to stalk you or anything.

I just didn't want to disturb you. It looked like you were in the middle of something personal."

"It's nothing. That woman used to work for me and she just lost her husband in a terrible industrial accident. She's going through a rough time and I'm supporting her. That's all. Did you want to talk to me about something? Why were you waiting for me? Is this about your club membership?"

She winces. "Actually....kind of yes and kind of no. It's.....about my husband. He's getting really defensive about the club.....and everything, really. He says....he says he wants to be present if I meet with anyone from the club or any man in a business capacity." She passes her hand across her eyes. "I'm at my wits' end about what to do about him—and I realize that I really need this club. I need the company of other people who are in the same income tier as I am—and he isn't. See? We've always kept our money separate. That was his idea from the beginning of our relationship—and now it's becoming an issue because I'm a billionaire and he isn't. Now he's saying he wants to be there when I come to the club or go to any club events or anything like that."

My eyes fall out of their sockets. "So let me get this straight. He wants to accompany you to the club.....what? To keep you under surveillance? Is that it?"

She flaps her hands. "Well.....yes....I guess so.....but actually to keep all of you under surveillance. He says he doesn't trust any of you not to make a move on me....."

"I would never make a move on someone at the club." I try not to snap, but this is the most insulting thing I've ever heard. "I would never make a move on someone in any business capacity, especially not someone who was married. We're going into business together,

Paige—and I treat my role at the club as a professional commitment, too."

"I know!" she groans. "I'm not suggesting that you don't. I'm not suggesting anything of the kind. I don't know what the heck is going on with him. I really don't. He's just completely lost the plot since we moved to New York. I really don't know what to do about him. Going along with this is my last-ditch effort to smooth things over. I wouldn't be bringing this to you at all if I thought there was any chance of reasoning with him."

I stare at her as the truth sinks in. She actually thinks the club members and I would go along with this—or maybe she already knows we won't and her husband is the one who thinks we would accept this.

I do my best to steady my voice. "I'm fairly certain the other club members won't agree to a non-billionaire coming into the club—especially not for something like this. We already have a policy to keep the club private. Non-billionaires are not allowed in the club—including the other male billionaires' wives. They've all accepted this. They realize we need a place where we can be ourselves with each other. Your husband is no different from them. He'll have to accept it, too."

"I know. I just.....I just thought I better ask....just in case there was any possibility."

"I will bring it up to the other officers, and if they decide to, we can float it on the agenda for our next meeting—and I have no problem with your husband attending our meeting on Thursday. I have nothing to hide and no plans to hit on you, either in his presence or out of it. That isn't what this is about."

She smiles for the first time. "I know—and thank you. I'm really sorry about this. This is the first time my personal life has intruded on my business. I won't make a habit of it."

I can only shrug. "Personal life and business have a way of intruding on each other. No one expects you to totally divorce yourself from your personal life. We all have personal issues that intrude and that's just the way it has to be." I hesitate. "It's more the way it's intruding than anything else."

"I know—and thank you—and I'm sorry. I'm doing my best to contain the situation—and I'll take all necessary steps to make sure this doesn't interfere with our deal."

"I hope not." I wait a second. "Is there anything else I can do for you? Did you get my information on the membership application and the gala invitation?"

"Yeah, I got it." She smiles at me. Her smile has a way of weaseling into my heart. She's one of the sweetest, most outgoing, genuine people I've ever met. She makes talking to her effortless. "Thank you. I.....I don't know if Trent will agree to go, but I'll try. I'm keeping my fingers crossed that this is all just growing pains and he'll come around to liking New York as much as I do."

"Let's hope so. I'm meeting the other club officers later today. I'll let them know about his request and I can give you their answer when I see you on Thursday."

"Thank you." She holds out her hand. "It was really great to talk to you again."

I shake her hand as politely as I can. "You, too. Have a good one."

We walk off in opposite directions. I'm on my way to the club right now anyway.

The guys are never going to go for this. I don't even have to ask except that I already promised her I would. That's the only reason I'm going to bring it up at all, I wouldn't waste my friends' time with this nonsense otherwise.

I enter the club building, jog up the stairs, and turn on the power and heater before the meeting. I check a few other things in the office, but Jackson's comments about doing another man's job come back to me. I shouldn't step on his toes.

I wasn't stepping on his toes. He doesn't care who does what jobs as long as they get done. He just doesn't want me to think I have to do everything—and I don't. I just like doing things for the club even if it's just the little things.

He comes in next and grins at me when he catches me coming out of the office. "Do I need to get stern with you?"

I make a face. "You're really taking this new fatherhood thing way too seriously, you know that? Save it for your kids."

He bursts out laughing. He's so much happier since he got married. He says, "Yes, Sir," and starts opening his laptop to go over the club's financials before the meeting.

We always keep officer meetings casual. We don't even sit down. We just stand and shoot the bull, cover whatever we need to cover, and talk about whatever.

Today's meeting will probably focus more on organizing the upcoming gala. That's Judah's department and he shows up next with a bunch of information about the caterers, the decorators, the servers, and the venue.

Rory, Dante, and Lane roll in next and we start talking about the gala. "Did you invite Paige?" Jackson asks me.

"Who's Paige?" Judah asks.

"She's a prospective member," I tell him. "And yes, I invited her."

"Is she coming?" Lane asks. "Did she RSVP yet?"

I take a deep breath. "I wasn't planning on bringing this up until the end of the meeting, but I might as well do it now. She hasn't RSVPed because she doesn't know yet if she's going to come. She doesn't even know yet if she's going to apply for membership."

"Why not?" Rory asks. "She sounded pretty excited about it when she showed up here the other day."

I sigh. "She was. Her husband is causing problems for her. He doesn't like her branching out, spending time with other people apart from him, and he seems to take issue with her success because he doesn't share it. They keep their money separate, so he doesn't qualify for membership. He's insisting that she doesn't come to the club without him present to police all of us and make sure none of us behaves inappropriately."

"You have GOT to be kidding me," Lane snarls.

"I know," I reply. "I feel the same way, but I told her I would bring it up with you and see what you say, and if you want to, you can bring it up with the membership."

"So some creep can come into our meetings and hover around like a predator and treat his wife like a criminal?" Judah snaps. "I don't hardly think so."

"Exactly," Jackson adds. "I might be inclined to make an allowance for him if he was doing this for any other reason than that."

"Do we all agree, then?" I ask. "Is any of you in favor of this? I don't even know why I ask."

"No," Rory interjects. "None of us are in favor of this. I'm not in favor of us even bringing this to the membership. It's insulting—to all of us—especially to Paige. I can't believe she's actually going along with this."

"She did say this is her last-ditch attempt to reason with him," I reply. "She said he's completely lost the plot since they moved to New York."

"It sounds like it," Judah mutters. "It sounds like he's lost a lot more than that."

I nod. "I'm meeting her for business on Thursday. I'll tell her your decision. Now can we stop talking about this and go back to more important matters? Paige's relationship with her husband is her own business. She can work it out for herself."

Chapter 5: Paige

I walk into the conference room at People, Inc. and burst into a grin when I see Kevin standing up to greet me. He's such a nice guy. I never have to worry about him doing anything underhanded. He's too genuinely interested in other people.

We've been emailing and phone calling back and forth ever since I met him on Monday. Now we're here to negotiate a deal between People, Inc. and SigmaTech.

We both beam at each other while we shake hands. I feel like we've known each other all our lives. I already know what he's thinking before he even says it and vice versa.

"Great of you to come in," he tells me and turns to Trent who enters the room behind me. Kevin holds out his hand. "It's great to finally meet you, too."

Trent glares at him and completely ignores Kevin's hand. "It *isn't* great to meet you," Trent snarls.

A few of Kevin's colleagues, assistants, and fellow executives gasp and their mouths fall open, but Kevin completely waves it off. He motions to the chairs across from him. "Let's sit down and talk about this. You said you were going to get your head of education on board...."

"This is Mike Reed." I introduce the man next to me. "He's in charge of SigmaTech's education division. He'll be overseeing our training coaches who will be instructing your courses." I hand over a binder full of plastic-covered sheets. "This is the syllabus for the training course you'll be running."

Kevin sits down on his side of the table. Mike, the other SigmaTech managers, and I sit down on our side. Kevin starts turning the binder pages and studying the contents. Trent takes a seat in the corner away from everyone else.

"How many coaches do you have available?" Kevin asks.

"Fifteen," Mike replies. "They're the only people qualified at this point to teach others how to use our equipment."

"Then I think the first order of business is to train another batch to expand the operation," Kevin suggests. "We're going to have hundreds of people going through this program once the military gets involved and we're the only organization contracted to train them. We'll need I'd say at least another forty trainers to start with—and we need to include hands-on experience with the equipment—for the trainers for certain to start off with."

"Absolutely," I tell him. "We completely agree. That's one thing we wanted to talk to you about. We understand the need to get these people trained and deployed with the equipment as soon as possible, but it's more important that we have an assembly line of trained personnel rolling out at the same rate as the equipment itself. It would be better to wait until we have all the infrastructure in place before we complete any of Diego's fulfilment contracts."

"My communication with him suggests he isn't ready to take delivery on the equipment yet anyway—and the military is going to take even longer to adopt this equipment than the civilian sector," Kevin replies. "We can get the initial trainer training out of the way, bring these trainers up to speed, and then start with the actual medical personnel who are going to be operating the equipment in the field.

That will give me time to recruit the right people who will be going through the program on the back end."

I can't help but beam at him. "That sounds perfect."

He bends over the binder again and talks while he flips the pages and reads. "The next question is compensation. How much are you asking to provide the coaches, the information, and the equipment?"

I frown at him. "I don't understand your question. We aren't asking anything."

He looks up. "Why not?"

"Because! We're making money hand over fist on these contracts. Every person you train and supply to go with this equipment is money in our pockets. We'll be able to sell ten times more with these trained operators on the same ticket—maybe even a thousand times more. Why would we charge you when you're basically advertising our product for us?"

He studies me across the table. "Okay. I didn't think you would see it that way."

I frown again. "You aren't charging us, are you?"

"Of course not. Why would we charge you when you're the ones who are making it possible for us to procure all these people for such lucrative positions? This deal is going to make us a mint."

I grin again. "That's the way we see it."

He raises his eyebrows. "Okay. I was not expecting that at all. I thought that's what we were here for—to arm-wrestle about how much each of us was going to have to pay for this deal."

I laugh and hold up my hands in surrender. "No arm-wrestling here. I'm a snowflake."

He laughs with me. "Great. We can resolve our differences peacefully without resorting to bloodshed."

"Absolutely."

"Then the question is when we can get started. I have the facilities and a bunch of people lined up who can act as student trainers for your coaches to train. We can start on that as soon as you're ready to send your coaches over."

"We're ready to start now," Mike tells him. "We have all the materials and our coaches are ready to start training whenever you are."

"Great. Why don't you send them over first thing Monday morning?" Kevin replies.

Now Mike is the one who raises his eyebrows. "That soon?"

"You said you were ready whenever we were—and we said we were ready whenever you were. We agree we need to get this going as soon as possible. Tell me now if you aren't going to be ready by Monday."

"Oh, no, we'll be ready." Mike puffs out his cheeks. "We better get back to the office and get started. We have a lot to do and not much time to do it."

I stand up and extend my hand to Kevin. "It's always a pleasure doing business with you."

He stands up to shake my hand. "Likewise. Let's meet on Monday to ink this deal. Then we can all start pulling for the finish line together and get it done."

"Great." I can't stop beaming at him. "Thank you for everything."

He squares his shoulders and his eyes dart to Trent standing up behind me. "I raised your concerns with the members of the club. They've decided not to adjust their policy to allow you to bring your husband to club meetings and private social gatherings. I'm sorry, but that's their decision. Our invitation to the gala still stands—and anywhere else the members are allowed to bring guests. We really hope you understand and we really hope we see you at the gala. The female billionaires will all be there with their husbands—some of whom are also club members."

"Really?" I exclaim. "That sounds incredible!"

He nods. "Melody Gottlieb is a billionaire and she's married to Niko Holloway. She inherited her father's empire after his death and now she runs it in her own right. The other billionaires' wives will all be there, too. Some are executives in other companies you might be interested in doing business. Jackson is right about you meeting Dante Helme. He runs a health care organization that might be interested in your equipment—and the officers and I want to sincerely invite you to apply for membership anyway. We all think you would be a real asset to the club and we want to see you get involved."

I blush at him again. "Thank you. That is very kind of you—and please let the officers know that we understand and we appreciate their consideration in this matter."

He addresses both of us even though Trent stands back there radiating hostility through the whole meeting. "I also want to offer my personal support if either of you needs any help settling into New York. It can be a big place and very intimidating when you first move here. Not many people in the club originally came from here. The rest of us had to go through the same adjustment period that you're going through now."

"Thank you," I murmur. "That means a lot."

Kevin turns to Trent. "I understand you may have gotten the wrong impression of my intentions toward your wife, Mr. Novak. I want to assure you that I meant nothing of the kind and my interest in her is strictly professional. I want to offer you my services. I run a personnel and employment agency that matches people to the right jobs in dozens of different industries. I want to offer you my help and support to find you a job you can get excited about and to help you succeed. I hope you'll feel free to call on me and make use of our services so you can thrive in New York the way you want to." He glances at me. "Have a good day. I'll see you on Monday."

He waves us out of the room and he and the other People, Inc. officers escort us to the lobby where we all shake hands and say good-bye—except for Trent, of course. He hangs back and doesn't shake hands with or speak to anyone.

"Can you believe the nerve of that cocksucker?" Trent snarls once we get outside. "He actually had the balls to insult me to my face!"

I spin around and stare at him. "What?! No, he didn't! He was super nice."

"He shoved it in my face that I don't have a job and he's gonna swoop down and be my guardian angel by giving me one. Can you believe that? What a prick! Well, he won't get away with it. If this is his way of stealing you from me, he has another thing coming."

My jaw hits the pavement. I actually stop in my tracks to stare at him. I get another sinking feeling in my gut when I hear the way he spouts all this poison about Kevin.

Kevin conducted himself with absolute impeccable professionalism during that meeting. Rarely have I met anyone who can act so exactly appropriately every single minute and at the same time put his counterparts so effortlessly at ease.

He's a master at handling people. He can joke around and keep it casual without ever letting his professional standards slip. It really is a pleasure doing business with him—and I get the sense that he acts that way toward everyone.

I saw him through the café window when he comforted that woman who lost her husband.

Kevin acted warm, caring, attentive, and even affectionate toward her without ever stepping out of line. Everything he did was strictly within the bounds of their professional relationship.

He can act like that with someone in a professional capacity because he actually cares about people. That's his job, but it's also his super-power.

That's why he offered to help Trent. Kevin realizes Trent is feeling insecure because he isn't succeeding. Kevin offered the one thing Trent most needs to get his confidence back—and Trent suspects Kevin of using this to undermine him.

I stand on the sidewalk watching Trent walk away from me to go get into his car—the car we brought from North Carolina. He's walking away from me in more ways than one. I'm watching my marriage fall apart right in front of my eyes.

Chapter 6: Kevin

I go around the gala ballroom shaking hands with everyone and hugging the women I know and am friends with. I greet Mckenna Pearson Metcalf. "Hey! You look outstanding!"

She blushes and kisses me on the cheek. "So do you. Thank you so much for your card. I really appreciate it."

"We're all thrilled that you're back on your feet." I look around. "Where's your husband?"

"He's over there hanging our coats in the coat room." Now she looks around. "Don't tell me you came without a date again."

I laugh. "No one wants to date me. Seriously, Mckenna. I'm a psycho behind closed doors. This is all just an act. Don't you know that by now?"

Jackson comes over to us just then, shakes my hand, and winds up hugging me, too, but I get distracted by another group of attendees showing up just then. I don't have time to talk to anyone right now. I'm too busy greeting people.

I get into a deep discussion with Niko about providing pilots, officers, and crewmembers for a new line of cargo ships he's acquiring.

"You're going global," I remark. "I'm only surprised it didn't happen sooner."

"Do you think you can hook me up?" he asks. "I have fulfilment contracts standing by and I have the ships to carry the goods. I just don't have any personnel."

"Didn't the previous owner have personnel? Why don't you offer to bring all those people back on board?"

"They're unionized," he tells me. "I would have to negotiate with the union if I did that."

"So what? So negotiate with the union."

He makes a face. "That's what I need you for. I'm no good at that."

"Oh, please, brother!" I chide. "You have your own unions driving your trucks all over the country. You negotiate with unions all the time!"

"Okay, so I'm not as good at negotiating with them as you are. I already know all the truckers' reps and everything. We're familiar with each other and understand each other. I don't know these people from a hole in the ground."

"I can do that. Then the union pays the recruitment fee so you don't have to."

He raises his eyebrows. "You don't say! I didn't know."

"Which union is it?"

"I'll send you all their information. I need these crews back on the job yesterday."

I clap him on the shoulder. "I got you. Leave it with me."

"Thanks, man. You're a lifesaver."

We both turn to greet Melody coming over to us right then. She has that gleam in her eye like she wants to talk business. She slips her hand through her husband's arm and arches her eyebrow at me. "Kevin."

"Melody. Why do I sense a business proposal coming on?"

She laughs. "I have no secrets from you."

"Do I need to put an absorbent pad in my underwear before I hear this?"

Both she and Niko laugh this time. "I think you better," he tells me.

Movement catches my eye just then and I spot Paige and Trent Novak entering the ballroom behind the other billionaires.

Paige looks absolutely regal in an off-the-shoulder white gown. It's simple, elegant, and shows off every majestic curve. Her jewelry sparkles in all the right places. Trent has to know his wife is one of the most stunning women in the room.

He looks pretty good in a tux, too. He's taller than she is with straight brown hair, brown eyes, and a strong, square jawline. He would look even better if he didn't let his hair grow so long. He looks like he's trying to make a statement by not cutting it.

She glows with pleasure when the billionaires she already knows go over there to greet her. They introduce her to their wives and they all start talking.

Trent doesn't look happy to be here. He eyes everyone with suspicion. The best possible expression he can muster is bland indifference to something that obviously means a great deal to his wife. What a chump.

I turn back to Niko and Melody to ask what her idea is. I'm sure it will be something spectacular. She's turning out to be one of the greatest business minds in the club.

I don't get a chance to say a word before Paige and Trent glide through the crowd in our direction. She smiles at me, but she doesn't extend her hand. I don't extend mine.

I wave between her and Melody. "Paige Novak, this is Melody Gottlieb, CEO of Paragon Holdings. Paige is CEO of SigmaTech and a prospective club member. You two should get to know each other."

Paige bursts with her usual gush of light and energy. She shakes Melody's hand. "Hi! It's so wonderful to finally meet you! Kevin has been telling me so much about you!"

"And this is her husband, Niko Holloway," I interject. "He's also a member."

Paige beams at him and shakes his hand, too. "Hello!" she exclaims. "I can't believe I'm actually meeting you both. This is like something out of a movie or something!"

They both smile at her. "I've been talking to Diego about your upcoming contract, Paige," Niko tells her. "He wants to include me in it to transport the equipment overseas and to the military bases he'll be delivering to."

Her eyes widen. "Really? I had no idea you all did so much business with each other."

"That's one of the purposes of the club," I tell her. "It's as much about networking and furthering our business interests as about socializing with each other and our families."

Paige opens her mouth to answer—and gasps. All color drains from her cheeks. "Oh, my gosh!" she husks. "Is that Mila Knapp over there? I'm her biggest fan!"

"She's Giovanni Nowaczyk's wife," Melody tells her. "He's over there. Would you like me to introduce you to Mila? She would love to meet you."

Paige's jaw drops. "Could you?! Really? Oh, my gosh! I'm a nervous wreck! I can't believe this! This isn't happening!"

Melody grabs her hand. "Come on. It's not that big a deal."

She tows Paige away and they head over to talk to Mila. Mila is in the middle of a conversation with Emberlynn Rhinehart—probably about Mila performing at the next MegaDome Experience.

Trent follows them over there, but he doesn't get involved in their conversation—or any other conversation. He doesn't engage with anyone. He just lurks in the background spreading creepy vibes everywhere.

"And they were never seen or heard from again," Niko murmurs.

I chuckle. "At least she came. I didn't think she would."

"I'll tell you one thing, my friend. If I knew something like this was going to make my wife this happy, there is no way on God's green Earth I would ever stand in her way of doing it. This dude isn't fit to be a husband if he could rob his wife of something she needs so badly."

I look away. "It isn't my business to comment on it."

"It's going to become our business if she joins the club."

"Well, she hasn't joined the club. She hasn't made any move to apply. This is the last event she'll come to as a guest. I won't invite her again. We won't see her again if she doesn't apply for membership."

"You'll see her again," he points out. "You're doing business with her."

I don't give myself the option to look at him. "That's true, but I probably won't see much of her after we ink the deal. She'll do her part and I'll do mine. Then we'll each do our parts separately. We won't deal with each other after that."

"It's a shame, though, isn't it?" He gazes across the ballroom at Paige, Mila, and Melody all talking together. Mila's blind eyes look off in the wrong direction, but she laughs and blushes as much as the other two. "She could have been great. It's a shame she doesn't join."

A few other people come over to us just then and our conversation shifts. I forget all about Paige, Trent, and everything else associated with them. I see them mingling with the other club members and their guests, but I don't talk to Paige or Trent again.

I'm on the other side of the ballroom refilling my champagne flute when Trent comes up to me by himself. I'm actually surprised he doesn't stay over there shadowing his wife every minute of the evening.

I don't say that out loud, though. I don't say anything to him. I can already see where this is going. His eyes flash with danger. He only left her alone so he could come over here and confront me while I'm by myself.

He steps up to me standing way too close. "You stay away from my wife. Do you understand?" he snarls. "I don't know what you think your money can buy you with every other man's wife, but you stay away from mine."

"I never did anything with your...."

He cuts me off by swiping his forefinger right under my eye. "Do you think I'm too stupid to see what's going on right in front of me? Did you sleep around with her already? Is that what you're doing while she's supposed to be at the office?"

I gasp in horror. "I would never do anything...."

"Don't lie about it!" he snaps. "I know you email and talk to each other all the time! She calls you from our apartment! Did you know that? She calls you right in front of me!"

"We're doing a business deal together, Mr. Novak! She calls me on business! I have never done or said anything with Paige that wasn't directly related to our business dealings. I don't see how you can accuse her...."

"I know what you're doing!" he fires back. "Don't think I don't know! You've had plenty of time to sneak out to each other's offices or some other place. How many of these guys even know what you're capable of? How many other women in this room have you screwed around with behind their husbands' backs?"

I gape at him in stunned disbelief. No one has ever accused me of cheating before—with anyone—certainly not with multiple women—the wives of my closest friends.

My blood runs cold at the thought. Who else is he telling about this? Is he out there telling every man in the club that I banged Paige on the side?

I swallow hard and do my best to keep my voice steady. "I assure you, Mr. Novak, I have never seen your wife anywhere other than in busy, public places. I have never even been alone in a room with her. You and your wife have been in New York for less than a week. We wouldn't have had time to do anything even if either of us wanted to—which we don't."

He glares at me. "You're a stinking, filthy, lying, backstabbing piece of shit. You stay away from my wife if you know what's good for you."

He barges away into the crowd. I cringe when I see him walk over to Paige, grab her arm, and pull her away from the conversation she's having with four other women. He can't possibly have a problem with that—but apparently he does.

He drags her to the exit. She protests all the way, but she doesn't fight him off—not in front of the whole gala. He marches her out into the hotel lobby and they don't come back.

I turn my back to the room and take a drink from my glass. I need to do something about this. I need to do some damage control to cope with his accusation. This could be disastrous for me if it got out.

Jackson comes up to me just then. He startles me by clapping me on the shoulder from behind and then stepping up next to me to refill his own glass.

"Hey, champ," he tells me. "This is a rocking party. The organizers really outdid them....." His expression darkens when he looks at me. "What's the matter? You look like you just got punched in the guts."

I swallow hard. I can't look at him. "I need to talk to you, Jackson."

"Okay. I'm standing right here. What's the problem?"

"No, I mean...I have to talk to you and all the other officers—right now—right this minute."

He scowls at me. He can look downright dangerous when he scowls like that, but his expression actually makes me feel better. He's taking this seriously—as seriously as I need him to take it. No one knows better how to deal with a serious situation than he does.

He dips his chin once. "Okay. Let's go."

He turns away. I toss down the rest of my drink, take a deep breath, and follow him out onto the ballroom floor. He rounds up Rory, Dante, Judah, and Lane in a heartbeat.

Jackson narrows his eyes at me when he returns with all of them following him. He leads the way into one of the hotel's back rooms adjacent to the ballroom. We keep extra suits and evening gowns in here in case something happens and one of the members or their wives needs to change.

"What's going on?" Judah asks. "Jackson said you wanted to talk to us urgently."

I can't stop my voice from shaking. "Trent Novak just accused me of cheating with his wife."

Rory gasps. "He did not!"

I nod fast. I can't look up from my trembling hands. "He accused me of cheating with all your wives."

Dead silence falls over the room. Then Lane bursts out laughing. "I'm sorry, man!" He presses the back of his wrist against his mouth, but he can't stop himself from laughing. "I'm so sorry! I shouldn't laugh, but Jesus! I mean....does he even know you? This is absurd!"

Some of the others bite back smiles. "We all know you wouldn't do that," Judah tells me.

I squirm inside my jacket. "I'm just telling you. I don't want you to find out from someone else."

"Lane is right," Jackson adds. "We all know you. This is ridiculous. It would be comic if it wasn't so outrageously insulting."

"I don't think you have anything to worry about," Dante tells me. "No one in the club suspects you of anything. We all know you would never touch another man's wife."

"I just....." I cover my eyes. "No one has ever accused me of anything like this before."

"He's out of his tree!" Lane counters. "He's obviously delusional. I mean....I could understand a man accusing *me* of cheating with his wife—or Giovanni—but you?! That's just...no. I mean....no. Not you. Anyone but you."

I find myself smiling at him. "Thanks, brother. That means a lot coming from you—all of you."

Judah claps me on the shoulder. "Your reputation speaks for itself. You've been living and doing business in this town for a long time. This yokel just rolled into town last week. He doesn't know you. We do. Shit, everyone in this town knows you. No one is going to believe this."

"It just....it bothers me. That's all."

"Of course it does," Jackson replies. "It would bother any of us to have someone accuse us of that—except maybe Lane here and he's a special case. The point is that we all support you. The fact that you're telling us proves your integrity is unimpeachable. You have nothing to worry about."

I shut my eyes and turn my head away. "Thanks."

Dante steers me toward the door. "Come on. They're gone now. You can go back to enjoying the gala. We've put too much work into this to let something like this spoil it for us."

We head back out onto the floor. Everyone is enjoying themselves, especially now that Trent isn't around casting doom and gloom everywhere.

I find it hard to get back into the party spirit. His accusation hangs over my head like a curse.

What if this ruins my deal with Paige? I'll be okay if it does, but this would be a black mark on my reputation even to have someone accuse me of cheating when I didn't.

Chapter 7: Paige

I try to tear out of Trent's grasp. "What are you doing?! What is the matter with you?! I was enjoying myself in there!"

"That's the problem," he growls back. "You enjoy yourself a little too much, I'd say."

"What are you talking about?! Let go of me, Trent! You're hurting me."

He drags me over to the car, pulls open the passenger seat and practically hurls me into the seat. "Get in the car, damn it!"

He slams the door in my face and gets behind the wheel. I don't want to go anywhere with him when he's acting like this. I especially don't want to go anywhere when he's driving under the influence of so much rage.

He tears off into the night, screeches around a dozen corners, and skids to a halt into our apartment building's underground parking garage.

He opens the passenger door and waves at me. "Get out."

"What is your problem?!" I snap in his face when I stand up in front of him. "You agreed that we would go to the gala! We were there less than half an hour and you pull something like this!"

"Do you think I don't know what you're doing behind my back?! Do you think I don't know you're sleeping around on me every day with God knows how many people?!"

My jaw drops. "What?! I never...."

"I saw the way you were all laughing and smiling and flirting with Kevin during your meeting! You flirted with each other right in front of me! I knew it—and you're such a whore that you did it right in front of me!"

"I never flirted with him—ever—and neither did he! He was just being nice! He had his company executives there and so did I! Don't you think one of them would have noticed us if we were behaving inappropriately?"

"So you take it out of the office and screw him behind my back! Don't think I don't know! How long has it been going on? You could have been doing it with every mail clerk in your company while you were supposed to be at work!"

"I never cheated—with anyone, Trent! I never looked sideways at another man—but I bet you did, didn't you? Is that what this is about? You want to screw around with other women so you're accusing me first? Is that it?"

"You fucking bitch!" he roars. "I gave you everything—and now you cut my nuts off for some cocksucker you just met! You think you're all high and mighty and no one is good enough for you but another billionaire! Is that what tonight was? You want to parade me around in front of the other billionaires to show them I'm your bitch?! Is that it?"

"Trent!" I scream. "I never did anything—with anyone!"

He points at me again. "You can never see him again. Is that understood? You can never see him—ever—or anyone else from the club."

"I have to see him, Trent. We have a signed contract with obligations on both sides."

"Then you'll have to quit the company. This bullshit has gone on long enough. You'll have to hand off to someone else. It's me or the company. You can't have both."

I gape at him in horror—and then my shock and upset turn to fury—cold, icy fury. I narrow my eyes at him. This has been coming for a long time. I just didn't want to accept that it had gone this far.

"I won't quit the company, Trent. I will never walk away from SigmaTech—not ever. You never loved me at all if you could ask me to make that choice. I understand that now."

"Then it's over." He turns away, storms off, and yells, "Have a nice life," over his shoulder. He doesn't go into the building. He strides out of the parking garage, up the ramp, and disappears into the night.

I stumble over to the elevator and push the button to ride up to the penthouse. I can't think or feel anything on my way up there.

I don't turn on the lights once I get inside. I stop in the middle of the living room and look out the big windows at all the lights of New York sparkling in front of me. They shine from millions of other windows in other buildings all over the city.

New York City. That's where I am right now. I made it big and now I'm here. No one can ever take this away from me, but it still stings. My marriage is over. Trent is gone. He won't come back even if he does. It's over.

He never cared about me. He never loved me. He never wanted me to be happy. He never wanted me to succeed. He never wanted me to be my best.

He only ever cared about the money—and maybe the sex. It was never about me. I see that now. He cared more about protecting his money from me.

Then he did absolutely everything to stop me from becoming the best version of myself, from becoming successful, and doing what I needed to make me happy.

He actually tried to stop me from socializing with other billionaires. I can't believe he's turning out to be such a psycho creep—and I married him. What does that say about me? I must really know how to pick them.

I love this apartment. I love everything about this life. I didn't let myself acknowledge that as long as he hung around to poison that for me, too.

I love living in a beautiful, stunning apartment with such a magnificent view. I earned this with the sweat of my brow. No one is going to take this away from me.

I'll be damned if I quit SigmaTech for some dope from the backwoods who doesn't know how to act in public. He's a loser. He doesn't even have a job and he thinks he can come into my life telling me what to do! Like hell.

I go up to my bedroom, change out of my gown, and get into my pajamas. I suppose I could go back to the gala alone. I wouldn't have to worry about Trent interfering with any of my conversations this time.

That doesn't matter because I'm going to apply for membership and I'm going to get in. I'm going to get to know all those people and share all their stories and their lives.

I'm sure some of them have gone through nasty divorces, too. They'll help me the same way Kevin did—and does. He's a nice guy. I like him a lot.

I like everyone from the club. The women are super nice, welcoming, helpful, and supportive. I feel like they're all my sisters already.

Even the ones who are stay-at-home mothers are super motivated, business savvy, and pursuing their passions. I love that about them. I want their energy to rub off on me.

I didn't find out what half of them do. Thanks a million, Trent. I'll never let him stand in my way again. I'm going to join the club. He can't stop me now. He'll never stop me from doing anything again.

I get into bed, open my laptop, and type into my browser search bar, *Divorce lawyers, Manhattan.*

Wouldn't you know it? The very first listing that comes up is Piper Legrange. Her profile says she's handled divorces for some of the richest, most powerful businesspeople in the Atlantic states area, including Judah Hayes's divorce. Now she's married to him.

I already know Piper. She's a wonderful person—very subdued, understated, and super nice. She'll be perfect to represent me against Trent.

I have no doubt he'll make trouble for me. He'll try to get my money even though he was the one who insisted we keep everything separate.

He even insisted on a pre-nuptial agreement that we would never be able to claim each other's money in the event that we split up. Thanks another million, Trent. You did me a massive favor.

I enter my details into Piper's appointment scheduler. The website asks for details of what I want to see her about, so I enter those, too. I can get an appointment with her for early next week. That will be perfect.

Making the appointment settles my mind enough for me to put my computer away, turn off the light, and go to sleep.

Chapter 8: Paige

The world looks like a very different place when I wake up alone in my big fancy apartment the morning after the Gala From Hell. Trent didn't come home. He's gone. He dumped me. Our marriage is over.

I collapse back on the bed, heave a sigh, and run my fingers through my hair. I guess I have no reason not to continue with my life.

I get up, take a shower, get ready for work, eat breakfast, and organize all my stuff to leave for the day. I plan to take another cab to the office. I really should change that and I don't want to drive in New York. This place is a zoo when it comes to the traffic.

I decide to hire a car to drive me around. What the hell. I might even hire a limo like some of the other billionaires do. Why shouldn't I? I can certainly afford it.

I don't have time to arrange it today, though, so I take another cab. I check in with Mike first. "How's the new trainer training is going over at People, Inc?" I ask.

He laughs. "That expression makes me laugh!"

I have to join in with the joke. "I think it makes everyone laugh—and it is the most fitting description for the program."

"That Kevin is something else, isn't he? Everyone is using that expression now." Mike puts his arm around my shoulders while we walk down the hall. "Everyone at People, Inc. is so awesome. Everyone over there is super nice, super helpful, and super enthusiastic."

"It comes from the top, doesn't it? I can't imagine Kevin running any business that did it any other way." I study him on the side. "Am I to understand that the training is going well?"

"It's going great! The trainees are practicing on the equipment and using it to test themselves. Later in the program, they'll get experience using it in clinical settings on real patients. The trainees will be able to see the results, interpret them, and contribute to diagnoses and treatment protocols with other health care professionals."

"That's perfect. I'm meeting Kevin later today. I'll tell him what you said. I'm sure he'll be pleased."

Mike stops in the corridor and gets choked up trying to control his features. "I was so worried about rolling out the trainer training so fast, but the folks at People, Inc. made it a pleasure. You tell him that."

"I will."

I go over to People, Inc. to see for myself how things are going. I meet up with Kevin there. "Mike was practically in tears when he told me how well things were going," I tell him. "I just had to see for myself, but he wasn't exaggerating. I couldn't be happier with the results."

Kevin looks deep into my eyes. "It's important to me that SigmaTech is happy with what we're doing on our end of the bargain. I want to hear about it immediately if you see anything about our process that doesn't meet your expectations."

I smile at him. "You will. We're thrilled with how you're handling your end. You've exceeded our wildest expectations. I have no doubt this program will be a success."

"Good. I want to make sure you and everyone at SigmaTech is confident in this program and that you trust it enough to include our people in your offering."

"We are and we do. You don't have to keep reassuring me."

"Okay." He nods. "I think I can start to accept that."

I laugh at him. "Your attention to this project is really heartening. Everyone at SigmaTech thinks you're the greatest."

He waves that away. "I'm just doing my job." He pretends to look around. "Where's your other half? Why didn't he come to chaperone you?"

I groan and roll my eyes. "We got into a massive fight last night when he took me away from the gala. He flat-out accused me of cheating with you and who knows how many other guys. He's out of his head. Anyway, he got the brilliant idea to make me choose between him and the company—and then he dumped me when I said I wouldn't quit. It's over." I try to shrug it off. "Anyway, I don't want to talk about that anymore. It's done and good riddance. I'm just really sorry you got caught in the middle of it all. That wasn't fair to you—especially considering the way he smeared your reputation and called your integrity into question. That was totally uncalled for."

He watches my reactions until I finish. "I'm sorry you're going through this—and I'm sorry I came between you and your husband. That was never my intention."

"You didn't!" I put out my hand to touch his arm, but I stop myself in time. I don't want anyone else getting any ideas. "I'm sure this had nothing to do with you. He came up with this ludicrous idea before he ever laid eyes on you. All I did was tell him that I met you as club membership officer and that you invited me to the gala. He ran with it from there. He wouldn't even listen when I told him that you invited both of us to come together. He's totally irrational—about everything—and he was like that before I ever went to the club. Anyway, let's talk about something else. I want to send in my application now. I want to go ahead and apply for membership."

"Great," he exclaims. "All the members are delighted to have you on board. They all think you're the greatest, too."

I burst out in blushing laughter. "I'm going to pretend you didn't just say that."

"I did say it. They all say it. They all think you're wonderful. We would love to have you—and you can make up for not being able to talk to people last night. A bunch of people there were disappointed that they didn't get to talk to you. We might have to organize another extra gala just for you."

I can't stop blushing at him. "Stop it. You would not."

"You're right. We wouldn't, but you have to join. We need you. We need you real bad."

I laugh again. "Okay. I better get out of here before I get myself in trouble."

"I'll walk you out."

I ride back to SigmaTech and hold a bunch of communications with Diego, Montgomery, and Niko Holloway. Our deal is proceeding more slowly but no less inevitably toward a successful conclusion.

Staying on with SigmaTech is the right thing to do. Everything that happens today confirms that. No way will I walk away now—not for some jealous idiot completely detached from reality.

Trent doesn't even know these people. He doesn't know their character. He has no right to accuse them of anything—or me of anything.

I spend the last hour of my day locating a limo service to drive me around. Three of them operate in Manhattan and one of them outright claims in its ad copy that it caters to members of The Billionaires' Club.

I decide to give that company a chance until I can confirm with the other billionaires that they actually use the service.

I can't believe what's happening to me when I sit down in the seat and the car glides away into traffic to take me home. I can barely hear or see anything happening outside this little bubble of luxury. I float in a halo of serene bliss. No one can bother me here.

I'm actually riding in a limo. This is my first time ever. Will I really be able to do this every single time? Why shouldn't I?

I might actually be able to get things done on my way to and from work. I might be able to take phone calls or check documents I need to brush up on before meetings. This is definitely a nicer way to drive around than taking cabs or driving with Trent.

The limo drops me off outside the building's main entrance. This is a new experience from riding up in the elevator from the parking garage. I'm not sure which one I like better.

Getting out in the parking garage will be better if it's pouring rain or snowing. I'll have to check with the limo service to find out if the cars even can go down into the garage.

I ride the elevator up to the penthouse. I try to decide on the way what to do with myself tonight. I have a bucket list of things I want to do in New York, including seeing shows, music, art, theater, comedy—the works.

I want to visit all the museums and see all the sights, but I might have to wait for one of my days off to do some of it. It's too late to go to any museums now.

I can't decide if I should go to a show or stay in tonight. Maybe I should take it slowly until things cool off with Trent.

I freeze the minute I walk into the apartment and hear a woman screaming in the background. I know that sounds. It's the unmistakable sound of a woman in the throes of sexual passion. The sound is coming from upstairs—from the master bedroom.

I pull my phone out of my purse and turn on the video camera to record this. I can't believe it. Trent better not be doing what I think he's doing.

The sound gets louder as I tiptoe down the carpeted hallway getting closer to the bedroom. I hear a few other women in there—and the rhythmic banging sounds of the bed slamming into the wall.

Trent snarls dirty talk in between thrusts. He calls the woman all kinds of filthy names. He never would dare to talk to me like that.

I hold up my phone and stop outside the bedroom door. Trent kneels between a woman's spread thighs while another woman straddle's the first woman's face. Two other women lay in a sixty-nine position next to them while Trent fingers the woman on the bottom.

I stand in the hall watching the whole scene on my phone. I'm recording this less than twenty-four hours after Trent broke up with me. He's in here cheating with four other women in our bedroom—the bedroom we were supposed to share.

The girl on the bottom that my so-called husband is doing it with mumbles something to the woman above her. They shift their position. The girl on the bottom pulls away from him, rotates onto her knees, and the woman on top lies down on her back.

The first girl backs up to Trent and he starts pounding her from behind while she devours the woman in front of her. The woman on her back starts screaming this time.

One of the others gets the brilliant idea to stand up in front of Trent, present her genitals to him, and rub his face into them while he does it with the other girl. He keeps drilling his fingers into the fourth woman like he has nothing else to do with his time.

The woman standing in front of him tosses her head moaning and shrieking. I could almost believe she's faking it to make it seem like this

is all so much sexier than it really is. It looks downright gutter-trash to m
e.

Her eyes float open and she happens to see me standing there with my phone out and the camera light turned on. The woman freezes and then gets Trent's attention. He doesn't stop pumping when he looks over, sees me, and bursts out in insane laughter.

"Take a good, long look, you worthless tramp," he snarls. "If you can do it with any other guys, I can do it, too."

I stare at him in stunned disbelief. He did not just say that. He is not in here whoring himself out to four women over some imaginary affair I had with someone else.

Actually, yes, he is. Trent did just say that and he is in here whoring himself out to four other women. He plunges straight back into eating the woman out while he fingers another and thrusts his meat into a third. He really is doing this.

He doesn't look at me again. I record them for another five minutes before I start feeling too sick to stand this any longer. I stumble back downstairs. I'm still carrying my purse and laptop case from work. Now what am I supposed to do?

I think fast on my way back down the elevator. I used to love that penthouse. I'll never be able to stay there again.

I'm the leaseholder on the apartment. Trent never would have been able to afford it.

He's such a stickler for us keeping our money separate that he wouldn't put both of our names on any lease. He always held the leases on all our apartments back home. He liked to lord it over me by calling them, "my house".

I get into a cab and tell the driver to take me back across town toward the SigmaTech building. I decide to tell him to take me to a hotel. I don't care which one.

I start thinking much more clearly once I get into the room by myself. First I cancel the lease on the penthouse. It has a two-week cancelation clause so I'll get my whole deposit and half the rent back.

Then I call a private security firm to go to the penthouse. I call ahead and get the manager to unlock the apartment so the security guys can drag my husband and his girls out of bed stark naked.

The building has a sophisticated security camera system and an app the tenants can use to monitor the entrance and all the hallways.

The manager explained to us when we moved in that the app was so we could see if a delivery person was coming toward our apartment or if we noticed an intruder who isn't supposed to be in the building.

Now I use the camera system to watch the guards march Trent and the four women out of the building. Then I double-check my appointment with Piper. We're still on. I don't need to show her the footage. I'll do that at our appointment.

Chapter 9: Paige

The building manager opens the door to a different but equally nice penthouse apartment and I walk in to take a look around.

This one is in a completely different building and has a completely different layout. Nothing about this apartment reminds me of the apartment I once shared with Trent.

The view from this apartment's living room is much nicer and includes Central Park from a different angle. The apartment is on the other side of the SigmaTech building so there's no danger that I'll run into Trent on my way to or from work.

I've already asked the manager about limos pulling into the building's parking garage. He says the other high-end tenants do it all the time—so I won't run into Trent anyway.

This apartment also has a terrace with a pool. The building runs the pool service, so that's included in the rent. I absolutely love the apartment. It's gorgeous and somehow even more comfortable than the other one.

I smile at the manager and tell him I'll take it. I transfer the deposit and the first four months' rent. Then we go downstairs to sign the paperwork. I'll move into the apartment over the weekend.

I have half an hour before my appointment with Piper, so I spend the time arranging a moving company to move everything out of the old apartment.

I plan to go over there after work today, pack up only the bare necessities I want to keep, and leave the rest for Trent. He can work it out for himself how to get everything out of storage and truck it all back to North Carolina if he really wants to keep the stuff.

I feel myself shaking on my way upstairs to Piper's office. I'm seeing a divorce lawyer. Terrific. I've been in New York less than two weeks and I'm already getting a divorce. This is just stellar.

At least I have a layer I know and like. Piper meets me at her office door, shakes my hand, and then hugs me. She pulls me down to sit on a couch in the corner.

"How are you doing with it all?" she asks.

I roll my eyes to heaven. "I guess it's better than staying with the bastard. Look." I show her the footage.

She raises her eyebrows. "Wow. Just...wow. You gotta hand it to the guy. He's a stud."

I have to laugh. "You got that right."

She leans back on the couch. She's so laid back about this that she puts me right at ease. "So how do you want to do this? Your pre-nup looks watertight, especially since he's the one asked for it. Are you worried about your money?"

"Not really. Most of my net worth is tied up with the company anyway. He wouldn't be able to get to it even if he wanted to. The rest is all separate. It always has been. He wanted it that way."

"Then what exactly do you want me to do for you?"

"Mainly I just want to keep you on retainer to handle the paper-work and make sure he doesn't end-run me with something I haven't foreseen. I mean, he already has end-run me with something I haven't foreseen. I don't want him to do anything else—like try to get alimony from me."

"Your pre-nup specifically forbids that," she points out.

"That doesn't make it foolproof, does it?"

"Why don't you send me over your financial records? Then I'll have a better idea of what he could get if he tried. If you're right that you're so well protected, then it's possible he might not get enough to make it worth his while. You mentioned in your first message that he doesn't have a job and isn't looking."

"He doesn't and he isn't. As far as I know, he's too busy nailing cocktail waitresses or whatever the hell they are."

She laughs. "Then he probably wouldn't be able to afford a lawyer, would he?" She smirks at me. "He definitely wouldn't be able to afford a lawyer who could beat me."

I find myself smiling back at her. "That's a relief."

"I know practically every lawyer in town. Why don't we just keep an eye on the guy and see what he does? He might fade away into the woodwork of history and you'll never have to worry about him again."

I snort. "That would be way too easy."

"Keep a good thought. It has been known to happen."

I hesitate. "You represented Judah, didn't you?"

She smiles and nods. "That's how we met. He was in the middle of a messy, high-profile divorce that turned into a nightmare for everyone. His ex turned violent against both of us and eventually got herself killed."

I look away. "I really hope that doesn't happen with Trent."

"Just remember that it almost never happens. Very few divorces end that way or even wind up in court. Even fewer end with one party paying the other alimony. You should also know that the vast majority of pre-nuptial agreements hold up in court. We hear a lot about the handful of agreements that fail. We don't hear about all the others that do their job and protect the parties involved. Even when they do fail, the court needs to see extenuating circumstances that would suggest the agreement was entered into under false pretenses, coerced, or one party has some reason to call the agreement into question. I don't see that happening here."

I shrug. "I can't help but think the worst. This whole move has turned out so disastrously opposite from what it was supposed to be."

"I understand." She squeezes my arm. "The good news is that you still have the club and all its members. You aren't alone. Judah isn't the only member of the club who has gone through a divorce. Some have gone through several."

"Great," I grumble. "I don't want that to be me."

"I'm sure it won't be. You couldn't possibly have known when you married Trent that you would become a billionaire and that he would have such a massive problem with it. Things get easier when you come into this world and everyone already knows you're a billionaire. Then no one can possibly have a problem with you working as much as you do and making as much as you do."

"But how am I supposed to know if someone is trying to use me for my money? How would I ever be able to trust anyone ever again?"

She smiles at me. "One way would be to get together with someone from the club. There are a lot of really nice single guys in the club. You wouldn't have to worry about them going after your money. They don't need it."

I get out of her office as quickly as I can and do my best to go on with my life. It's a lot easier once I move into my new penthouse and don't see Trent around or anything that reminds me of him. He's never set foot in this apartment.

Kevin responds to my application later that day and invites me to come to the club the next afternoon as a guest to meet and greet everyone to see if I really want to join and if they really want me to join.

He assures me that this is a normal part of the application process and not anything the club members are specifically doing to throw obstacles in my way.

Chapter 10: Paige

I get another load of butterflies in my stomach on my way into The Billionaires' Club meeting. I'm sure everyone knows by now what's going on between me and Trent—or what's *not* going on between me and Trent.

I climb the stairs and get a very different reception than last time. Kevin and four other men stand there waiting for me.

"It's great that you finally made it," Kevin tells me. "This is Dante Helme. He's our current club president."

I shake Dante's hand. "It's nice to meet you. I've heard a lot about you. Some people around here think we should be doing business together."

He grins at me. "Some people around here have been telling me the same thing. We should talk."

Kevin introduces me to Judah Hayes next. I already know Lane Prince and Jackson Metcalf. "I hope you don't mind that Piper told me about your situation," Judah tells me. "She said I would be able to commiserate with you and support you."

"Thank you," I murmur. "I really need that right now."

"I'm sure your situation won't wind up as badly as mine did."

"I hope not—and I don't want to spend all my time at the club talking about that."

"Tell us how your deal with Kevin is working out," Jackson prompts.

I start telling them about the trainer training program and a few other details of my business and our position.

Diego comes over in the middle of this conversation and some of the others split off to talk to other members. Diego, Kevin, and I wind up talking about the SigmaTech offering and how we can package everything into one lump to make it more appealing.

"My clients overseas will definitely be more interested in the package if trained personnel are involved," Diego tells us.

"Could you bring the new customers on board first?" Kevin asks me. "We could drive up our market position if we build a waiting list of interested parties and new prospects have to get in line."

"Great idea!" I exclaim, and this time, I forget to stop myself from grabbing his arm. "We should merge! We should combine your company and mine! We should make it all one thing!"

"Hold up there, jumping bean," he tells me. "Just hold your horses one cotton-pickin' minute. People, Inc. covers a whole lot of industry staffing requirements. SigmaTech couldn't acquire all of that and you wouldn't want to. We could talk instead about merging my education and training department and infrastructure with SigmaTech, but not the whole thing."

I frown. "Oh, right. What was I thinking?"

"It's a good idea. We can definitely explore it further."

Diego raises his hands. "I think I'll just back away slowly....."

Kevin and I both laugh. Diego grins at us and goes over to the buffet to get himself something to eat. That leaves me and Kevin alone.

"Don't you want to talk to Dante?" he asks. "I'm sure you didn't come here to talk to me."

"Of course I did. I like talking to you."

He colors. "You know what I mean. You didn't come here only to talk to me."

"I'm not only talking to you. I'm only talking to you now, but I haven't been. Isn't that what we're here for—to talk socially?"

He shrugs. "I suppose so."

"Tell me more about yourself. I don't know anything about you. You know everything about me."

He smiles at me. "Not everything."

"You know enough. Where are you from originally?"

"Boston. My family is the Boston Abernathys. My mom was Bella Abernathy. She married Congressman Walter Drake's son Doyle Drake, which is how I came to have a different last name."

"I've never heard of the Boston Abernathys."

He bursts out laughing. "You're the first person I've ever met who hasn't heard of them. You really are a hick, aren't you? The Abernathys are a wealthy family. They're in the habit of donating to all the Ivy League colleges, national election campaigns, and founding think tanks for everything."

"Wow," I exclaim. "You said you ran away from all of that."

"I didn't run away. I walked away in a calm, stately, dignified manner."

I laugh along with him. "Oh, of course. Excuse my mistake. So what happened?"

"Nothing. I decided I wanted to become as filthy rich as the rest of my family, but I didn't want them to help me do it or pay my way or support me with a trust fund."

"Did you have a trust fund?"

"Of course. My grandparents set up a huge trust fund for me when I was born. It took me almost five years to convince them to dismantle it and put the money into one of their other endowments. I told them they could call it a donation if they really wanted the tax break."

"How did they take it?"

"They didn't like it, but I told them I would never touch a penny of their money as long as I lived. My dad was the one who finally came around and started to understand why I had to do it this way. He convinced my mom and they helped me to convince my grandparents to go along with it."

"So what happened when you walked away in a calm, stately, and dignified manner?"

His eyes twinkle and his cheeks flush again. He's actually really handsome when he smiles like that. He's handsome all the time—and he's an amazing, sweet, and considerate person. He is definitely one of the really nice single guys in the club that Piper mentioned.

"I left home, got a job as a dishwasher in a pizza parlor down the street from Harvard, and paid my way through school," he replies.

I gasp and my mouth falls open. "You went to Harvard?"

"No," he murmurs. "I went to Bunker Hill Community College. Then I transferred to Duke, but I only got a bachelor's degree. I never went any further."

"How did you found People, Inc.?"

"I actually started the company while I was working at the pizza parlor. I worked my way up to being one of the line prep cooks and then I became the nightshift manager. The owner needed more people to come on board and work. He couldn't find anyone, so I found them for him. I was in the middle of talking to one of my roommates who also needed a job. Our conversation got interrupted, and like magic, I saw an ad for a recruiting company on TV right at that moment. I looked into it and I found out that the company charged both the personnel and their clients for every placement. The company was dinging both sides in the transaction—and both sides were going for it. The client companies were happy to pay a headhunting fee and the new hires were happy to pay for the placement. I told both my roommate and the pizza parlor owner that I would be charging them a fee and they were both fine with it. The rest is history. I never would have believed I could make money that way, but it worked. The really cool thing was that I already knew everyone in town. I already knew who was looking for a job in what fields. I knew businesspeople who were looking for specialist personnel with specific training. All I had to do was introduce everyone to each other. It was too easy—and I got paid for it. The more people I placed, the more people I met, and the more people I met, the more people I knew in every company on the block. It avalanched into something huge until I was procuring whole workforces—like I'm doing with Niko now."

"That sounds amazing."

"How did you found SigmaTech?"

"I had a younger brother...."

"Uh-oh," he interrupts. "It's never a good sign when someone talks about their family members in the past tense."

"Exactly. He was born with a rare congenital blood anomaly. It was untreatable because the medical world hadn't come up with the equipment to treat his condition. The equipment hadn't been invented yet. No one had even thought about how to invent it yet. Everyone just put the whole idea in the too-hard pile. My brother died at the age of eleven after living his entire short life in agony. It was absolutely miserable for him to go through that and miserable for me, my sister, and my older brother to watch this poor kid suffer the tortures of the damned just to stay alive."

"Wow," Kevin murmurs. "That sounds terrible."

"It was—so it really got me thinking. I spent most of my childhood doing research on his condition and a whole bunch of other conditions with the same problem. The medical professionals knew what they needed to do to treat these conditions, but no one had developed the equipment to carry out the procedures."

"What kind of procedures are we talking about?" he asks. "You're going to have to forgive me. My thing is people. I don't do equipment and medicine and incurable diseases."

I wind up laughing. "It's okay. You have your superpower and I have mine. For example, my brother had a certain anomaly in his bloodstream that caused his white blood cells to mistakenly attack his red blood cells. The white blood cells wouldn't just envelop the red blood cells and remove them—which is what white blood cells are supposed to do. The white blood cells would deform and damage the red blood cells so they would continue to float around in his bloodstream causing problems in all his organs and muscles. It never got bad enough to kill him outright. It just caused widespread organ and tissue damage that got steadily worse over the course of years until his body eventually completely broke down. It was an excruciating way to die. But anyway, the doctors could have prevented that by putting him on a blood filtration system that removed the misshapen red blood cells. It's a modified form of dialysis, but it requires completely different machinery that puts the red blood cells through a centrifuge, separates the healthy red blood cells from the damaged ones, and removes the damaged ones."

Kevin raises his eyebrows at me. "You say that like you actually accomplished it. You say that like you actually developed this machine."

"I did. We've used it successfully to treat forty people with the same condition. I just developed it fifteen years too late to save my brother."

He shakes his head. "Dang. I am seriously impressed."

"Anyway, that led me to develop all this other equipment. Some of it is just prototypical next-generation upgrades on the equipment the medical field already has—with a lot of improvements, of course."

"Now I feel really inferior. That is one hell of a story."

"No way. SigmaTech wouldn't be able to function without your training program."

Dante comes over to us just then. "Is this a private conference or is anyone allowed to interrupt?"

"We're in a public place," Kevin tells him. "It isn't private."

Dante turns to me. "So....Paige....."

I laugh. "Dante Helme, I presume."

He laughs, too. Kevin touches my arm. "I'll leave you two alone. It was great talking to you, Paige. See you both around."

He walks away toward the buffet to intercept Niko. Dante and I start talking about my equipment, but I can't help glancing in Kevin's direction every now and then. I admire him for sticking to his principles and walking away from his family's money.

I admire a lot of things about him. He sure is nice. I wonder why he's single.

I don't actually even know if he's single. All our conversations have been totally professional and platonic. He might have a girlfriend. He might even be married, but he doesn't wear a wedding band.

He's nice. He's perfect. I could definitely get on board with doing something with him.

Chapter 11: Kevin

I shake hands with four different HR managers and migrate to a different table in the convention center. I meet people I know everywhere and they all want to introduce me to more people they know.

I meet up with Carlton James and Isaac Antonio Basrad. They shake my hand and start asking me about some big employment contracts they need staff for. We exchange contact details and I turn around to cross the room.

I stop dead in my tracks when I see Paige coming toward me. "Hello, stranger," she greets me. "I didn't know you were going to be here."

"I didn't know you were going to be here, either. It's great to see you. Are you just hobnobbing with the locals or are you here for some specific reason?"

"Just hobnobbing....getting to know people....This is a networking event, isn't it? I'm networking. How about you? Don't you already know everyone on Planet Earth?"

I laugh. "Not quite—but I'm getting there. I don't know *him*." I point to some random guy across the room and then look around. "I do know pretty much everyone else in this room, though.

She beams at me. "I'm sure you do. You're the man to know."

"Did you get my information welcoming you into the club?"

"Yeah, I got it. Thank you—and thank you to all the members. I'm thrilled."

"You're gonna be great. We couldn't be happier to have you with us."

"I'm looking forward to my next gala and wiping the last one from long-term memory storage."

I nod. "You'll have to find yourself a date. Something tells me you won't want to hire a male escort."

She grins at me. "No, I won't. I'll have to find just that right special someone."

I start to smile back at her and then I notice the way she's looking at me. Is she trying to send me a message? Does she think I might be that special someone?

She is definitely a special someone, but she's off limits. She's still legally married for a start. I can think of a dozen other reasons right off the top of my head why getting involved with her would be the worst idea ever.

Jefferson Winkler accidentally bumps into me just then, turns around, and his eyes go wide when he sees who it is he just bumped into. He's the executive in charge of HR at Surge systems.

He starts talking to me about their current staffing crisis, and the next time I look up, Paige is gone.

I really don't want to turn what is now a very profitable and comfortable platonic working relationship into an awkward, sub-text-charged, one-sided attraction on her part. That would be terrible.

Jefferson talks to me for an hour. He simply will not leave, not even when other people come over to greet me and tell me they want to talk to me about their needs, too. Everyone needs staff. Everyone always needs staff.

I finally tell Jefferson I have to go, give him my email address, and tell him to send me the list of everyone he wants. I get out of the convention center and head down the block. I haven't arranged for my limo to come and pick me up yet.

I'm supposed to go back to the event, but I need to take some notes on my phone about all the people who approached me today. I need to follow up with them and I don't want to forget anyone.

I stop there, pull out my phone, and tap out a hasty list of names and the companies connected each person is connected to. I can check the rest later.

I finish, put my phone in my pocket, and look up to see Paige coming up the street from somewhere. "Leaving so soon?" she teases.

"I think I need to download my brain into a computer. I have too many names and information floating around in there."

She laughs. "Let me take you out to lunch."

"I don't think that's a good idea....."

She stops in front of me and levels me with a direct look. I see in that moment that she really is interested in me. She only holds eye contact for a split second before she moves in and kisses me. I don't see it coming fast enough before her lips land on mine.

They feel silky smooth and magically soft, but some part of me already knew this was a bad idea. I push her away, but I make sure to do it as gently as possible. I take hold of her arms, hold her there, and move my head back so she can't follow it up by kissing me again.

"Whoa, Nelly!" I exclaim. "Just...whoa! Don't do that."

She only smiles at me. "I think you're the greatest, Kevin. I think you're sweet, kind, considerate, friendly, and I think you're incredibly attractive. I like you. I just want you to know that."

"I like you, too, but....." I struggle to clear my head. "You're still legally married, remember? You're on the rebound. I couldn't take advantage of that while you're vulnerable."

She laughs. "I'm not vulnerable, Kevin. I think you're a very special person and I like you. That's all."

I try to shake my head. I let go of her arms so I'm not touching her anymore. I take a step back to put some distance between us.

"I think you're a very special person, too, and incredibly attractive and appealing, but you're going through a rough time right now. You're going through a messy divorce. I couldn't take it further while that's going on. I'm sorry."

She only smiles, kisses me one more time very lightly on the lips, and murmurs, "Let me know if you ever change your mind."

She walks off toward the convention center and leaves me with my head reeling. Holy Christ—she kissed me!

I get the hell out of there, call my limo driver, and get him to take me home for the day. I need to be alone while I clear my head.

She's gorgeous—and we obviously have chemistry. I told myself she was just friendly and we got along well. We match each other's sense of humor and we speak each other's language in business. That's all—or I thought that was all.

What if all of that really was chemistry between us? Is that what made Trent so mad—because he saw chemistry between us? What if Paige and I really were flirting across the negotiating table?

I never would have flirted with a married woman—or any woman I was in a business negotiation with. I wouldn't cross that line.

She acts that way toward everyone, not just me. She acted that way toward Dante. She acts that way toward all the guys in the club.

They don't think she's flirting with them because she isn't. It's just the way she is. She really is just super outgoing, warm, and friendly.

She kissed me. Crapola. Now what am I going to do? I can't pretend that this is all platonic anymore. What if this ruins our deal? What if this spoils the whole arrangement between SigmaTech and People, Inc.? That would be terrible.

I hide in my apartment for the rest of the day and don't come out until it's time to go to work the next day. I have to endure a meeting with Paige this afternoon to discuss our mutual offering we plan to put together.

The package will include a recruitment and training fee for People, Inc. on top of SigmaTech's asking price for the equipment. The whole package will roll out together so we can start putting her equipment and my people on the market.

I stumble through the morning and get progressively more nervous as the meeting time draws closer. How will she act toward me now?

I take four other People, Inc. staff with me to the meeting so I don't ever wind up alone with her. She won't be able to do anything here. I just really hope she doesn't act inappropriately or make any suggestive remarks. I cringe at the thought of seeing her.

I hate that I have to feel this way about her. Things were going so well between us before this.

The People, Inc. team drives over to the SigmaTech building this time. Paige, Mike Reed, and two other SigmaTech executives meet us in the lobby.

I suffer a profound wave of relief that she's bringing her own people with her. I don't have to worry about the SigmaTech people thinking I brought a bodyguard to stop her from making another move on me.

We walk into the conference room and Paige and I sit down across from each other as usual. Nothing has really changed except that everything has changed.

She smiles across the table from me, but it's the same smile she used to give me before. It's a friendly smile of one platonic colleague to another.

Can I really hope that she'll just drop the whole thing and let us go back to being just good friends? I really, really hope she does.

"So....." she begins. "Let's talk about our offering. How much are you planning to charge for your finder's fee?"

I push a piece of paper across the table. "This is our usual pricing structure. We offer a discount for large employment contracts involving hundreds or thousands of employees. Of course we charge extra if the person or people have specialized training or industry-specific skills—so I would say anywhere in this range here." I use my pen to draw a bracket around the top tier of our price hierarchy. "Let me know if you think that's unreasonable."

"I think it's very reasonable for you to expect to charge top dollar for these people since no one else in the industry has these skills or this equipment. I think it's perfectly reasonable for you to command a premium even above this—and we have a waiting list of prospective customers now. That will drive the price up."

I raise my eyebrows at her. "You do? You didn't tell me that."

"You were the one who suggested that we start a waiting list. We're considering doing this on a bid-contract basis where we bid out production batches of our equipment. The customers who are willing to bid the highest will get their contracts fulfilled first. Customers who are in a hurry or have deadlines to meet will have to pay more to meet them."

I frown at her. "So.....you aren't concerned about pricing yourself out of the market?"

"I don't see that we're pricing ourselves out of anything. We'll fulfill each contract in descending order of price. My concern with your fees was that they would add too much to our asking price, but they aren't doing that. I don't see that we'll have a problem finding buyers for these packages. Your fees are within our projections—very much within our projections. We might even be able to drive the price up and split the difference between ourselves by asking for higher bids. The customers could get into a bidding war over who want the first consignments of equipment and personnel."

"That is totally not what I expected you to say—but okay. Twist my arm. You talked me into it."

She laughs and her eyes twinkle. She looks genuinely happy to talk to me—and to talk to me in a totally platonic way. She doesn't use any subtext or hidden messages at all.

None of the people around us see anything different about our interaction from every other time we've met in a business setting.

We go over SigmaTech's base asking price—the price the company would have asked if they didn't use this bid-offer system.

"Let's say we take your highest fee as our starting point and add that to our asking price," she suggests. "That will be the very lowest bid we'll accept. We won't accept or fulfill any bid below that, but we won't announce this price to anyone that this is our bottom line. We'll just take their bids and see how much higher they can go. I think these bids will come in much higher than that and then we can think about raising our baseline price in accordance with demand."

I raise both hands and lean back in my chair. "You're the boss here. I'll go along with that. I mean, if it doesn't work out, we'll just fall back on our original pricing structure, right? We won't have lost anything."

She smiles at me. "This waiting list was a stroke of genius on your part. We wouldn't be in a position of being able to call for bids if we didn't have the waiting list. I think this is going to be even more lucrative than we thought."

We both stand up and shake hands. All of us shoot the bull for a while before she and her team escort us out of the building. That went so much better than I dared to hope.

Thank all the stars in heaven she plans to drop it and not come after me again. I couldn't handle that—not with so much riding on this deal.

Chapter 12: Kevin

I get through the rest of the week and wrapping up a bunch of SigmaTech training courses and starting new ones. I have to deal with Paige almost every day, but she never even hints that she came onto me. She completely lets it go, thank God.

I actually start to look forward to seeing her at the club on Friday. I'm standing across the room talking to Rory and Giovanni when she comes in. She walks over to Lane, Dante, Derek, and Jackson. They all start to talk.

I'm in the middle of my own conversation, so I don't go over there. I don't get anywhere near Paige until much later.

"We couldn't file for divorce until we had already been separated for six months, so we just filed last week," she tells them. "Piper says we should have the whole thing finalized by the end of the month if Trent keeps behaving himself."

"Congratulations," Lane tells her. "Do you have your next conquest lined up?"

"Lane!" Jackson snaps. "Watch your mouth."

"I'm just saying she'll be a free agent." Lane turns back to her. "Any guy would be lucky to get together with you. That's all I'm saying."

She beams at him. "Thank you. I'm feeling lucky."

"I didn't want to bring this up, but did you see the article he did for Newstalk?" Derek asks.

She frowns at him. "What's that?"

"It's a tabloid that covers the dramatic personal lives of the rich and infamous." He navigates to something on his phone and hands it to her. "He's telling everyone you cheated on him as soon as you rolled into town."

She groans and rolls her eyes. "I'm going to have to refute that."

"How can you?" Jackson asks. "You can't bring out witnesses to testify that they didn't sleep with you."

She hands Derek's phone back to him, pulls out her own, and shows them something on it. "I took this the day after the gala—less than one day after he told me it was over. He won't be able to prove I cheated because I didn't."

"What a whore," Lane remarks. "I take back what I said about your next conquest. Now you can go out and start having five-somes with hot strippers, too."

She laughs at him. "I think not. Thanks for the offer, though, but I'm looking for someone special—someone I can really commit to—someone I can trust as much as he trusts me."

"I'm sure you'll find the right guy," Dante tells her. "You deserve it."

I stand off to one side listening to the other guys banter with her. I wish I could go back to that. I'm jealous—and not of their banter. She's talking about going out with someone new. She's talking about going on with her life and finding another guy—the right guy.

She said she thought I was special, but she'll never initiate again. I don't want her to—but it sure would be nice.

I find myself studying her from afar. I check her out much more closely this time. She comes to the club in another blazer, tight slacks, high-heeled ankle boots, and a short, tight shirt pinched at the waist.

She has a body to die for. I remember what she looked like at the gala. She looked absolutely succulent. I can just imagine running my hands down those swooping hourglass curves.

Her magical, infectious smile lights up her small, cherubic face. Her short hair and tasteful jewelry make her look deliciously feminine in a chic, modern, no-nonsense way. She's one of the hottest women I've seen in a long, long time.

She also has an absolutely adorable personality. She's bubbly, vivacious, laughs and jokes easily, and she's so easy to talk to. She gets along with everyone.

Someone would have to be a real dirtbag like Trent to have a problem with her. No one has a problem with her. Everyone loves her. What's not to love?

I shouldn't be thinking about her like that—but I am. That's the truth. I'm thinking about her like that a lot. I can't stop myself, now that I've started.

I actually catch myself thinking about kissing her, touching her... .and imagining what she would look like in bed.

I imagine her screaming in ecstasy, her beautiful body arched and shivering with passion, her soulful eyes rolling into their sockets as her toes curl in luscious climax.....

I really need to stop thinking like that. I don't want to walk around the club with a hard-on, especially not when she's standing here in the same room with me.

I start to turn away. It's almost time to shut down the club meeting anyway. A commotion draws my attention back to the group. My heart stops when Trent walks in.

Paige's happy smile evaporates into a cold, brutal mask of pure venom. "What the hell are you doing here?" she snarls.

He strides toward her and holds out his hand. "Come on, baby. Can't we at least talk about this?"

"You want to talk?" she snaps. "After you fucked four women in our bed—at the same time?! You're out of your mind! Get out of here, Trent!"

Dante cuts between her and Trent to stop him from getting near her. "You shouldn't be in here, man. The security guard at the door shouldn't have let you inside. You need to leave."

I cross the room in a heartbeat, but Jackson and Judah get there first and step in to back up Dante. I won't be able to do anything the three of them can't do. Even one of them would be able to squash me.

Trent struggles to get past them so he can get near Paige. He keeps stretching out his hand to her. "Come on, Paige. I love you! We've gone through too much together to just throw it all away."

"*You* threw it away, you sleaze!" she counters. "You were the one who dumped me and you were the one who cheated on me less than twenty-four hours later! I never did anything to you, Trent! I did everything for you and this is how you treated me—and now you're out there trashing me in the press on top of it all! You're the asshole here—not me!"

"I know, baby. Just...just give me another chance."

"Never!" she snaps. "You're done. Get out of here."

He doesn't back off. Jackson and Judah grab Trent by the arms and start hauling him toward the exit. I make a quick call downstairs to the security guards who should have stopped Trent from entering the club in the first place.

Four of them show up to drag Trent out of the building. I follow them to make sure he actually leaves. The seven guys park him on the sidewalk and line up to block him from the entrance.

"Leave now before I call the Police," I tell him. "If you ever come back here or to any other club function, I'll have no choice but to have you arrested for criminal trespass, harassment, and stalking. Is that clear?"

He glances around at all of us, hangs his head, and leaves without a word. The guys and I watch him out of sight. What a sad, pathetic excuse for a man—showing up here and embarrassing Paige and himself like this.

I wait a little longer and turn around. Jackson, Judah, Dante, and the four security guards still barricade the club entrance. "Which one of you was on duty at the door just now?" I ask.

The guards exchange glances and then point at a young Latino guy with buzzed hair and a short-clipped mustache. "Elijio was."

I turn to the guy. "It's your job to stop random strangers from barging into the club. What happened? How did that guy get inside?"

Elijio's eyes dart from one person to another. He looks like he's about to run away.

"Answer him, homey!" a black guard named Donny snaps. "You're making all of us look bad."

"Were you standing on guard at the door like you were supposed to?" Jackson demands. He's getting his dangerous face on now. "Tell the truth."

"Yes, Sir!" Elijio exclaims. "I was there. I wouldn't leave."

"Are you sure about that?" Jackson asks. "You didn't just sneak around the back to take a piss or take a hit off a joint or maybe snort a few lines? Is that what happened?"

"No, man!" Elijio squirms in front of Jackson. Anyone would. "I don't do drugs."

"I think I know what happened," another guard interjects. He's a young white kid named Ricky. "He paid you off, didn't he? He greased your palm and you let him in. Come on. Where's the money?"

Ricky storms up to Elijio and starts patting down his pockets. Ricky sticks his fingers into Elijio's pockets and starts turning them out.

Elijio goes ballistic, tries to slap Ricky's hands away, and backs up to get away from him. The other two guards move in, and before any of us can say a word, Donny and another white guy named Frank pin Elijio against the wall.

Ricky goes through his pockets and fishes out five nice, new, crisp hundred-dollar bills.

"Where did you get that, huh?" Ricky bellows in Elijio's face. "Huh?! Where did your bitch-ass get that money?! You didn't just happen to bring it with you when you left the house this morning, you ghetto piece of trash!"

"Okay, boys." I pull Ricky away. "Let him loose."

Ricky throws the money in Elijio's face and spins away. "We had nothing to do with this, Mr. Drake. I swear it. You put any of us on the door. No one will bother you. You have my word on that."

"I believe you, Ricky. Thank you for getting to the bottom of this. Donny, you stand the first shift on the door. Ricky, you and Frank go back to your posts. The club is almost done for the day anyway. Elijio, I think you better take your money and go home. I'll call your supervisor in a few hours and tell him what happened."

Elijio scrambles to pick up his money and slinks off in a different direction. The other guards glare at him before they return to their posts. Donny takes his position at the door.

"Well, that's a first," Jackson remarks.

"We should just stick with these three guards from now on," I tell the others. "We know them and they know us. We can trust them. It will be better to move forward with fewer guards than to bring in new people who might pull something like this again."

"I can roll with that decision." Dante turns to the other two. "Are you?"

Jackson and Judah both nod. "We'll tell Lane and Rory what's going on. I'm sure they'll be fine with it after today."

We all go inside. The other billionaires are gathered around Paige. She looks shaken and she keeps passing her hand across her forehead.

I stay away from her until the club meeting breaks up. I catch her by herself before she leaves. "Are you okay?" I ask.

"Yeah," she murmurs. "I'm really sorry about this."

"Don't be. It wasn't your fault. You handled it perfectly by not waffling and giving him false hope about taking him back."

She makes a face. "I can't get this divorce over fast enough."

Chapter 13: Paige

"Oh, my God!" I moan. "There he is! He's coming toward us!"

"Stay calm," Piper murmurs in my ear. "Don't do anything. Try not to show any sign of fear. They can sense it."

I laugh nervously. "I'll hide behind you. You can protect me from him."

She joins in the joke. She's half my size.

She doesn't have a problem turning around and extending her hand to Trent when he rolls up outside the New York City Courthouse.

"Thank you for coming, Mr. Novak," Piper tells him. "I'm sure we can all agree it's best if we get through today's proceedings in as civil a manner as possible. Don't you?"

He nods, shoots me a glance, and looks away.

Piper waves toward the steps leading up to the building entrance. "Shall we?"

I make sure to keep her between me and Trent on the way inside. We have to stand around for a while before our appointed time to appear before a judge.

Another attorney doesn't show up to represent Trent. It looks like Piper was right. He couldn't afford to hire anyone, especially not someone as good and as well-respected as Piper Legrange.

Our appointment time finally rolls around and the three of us enter the courtroom. I'm a bundle of nerves, mainly just from being in the same room with Trent. I keep expecting him to try to grab me or make another scene.

The judge barely looks at us. He calls the hearing to order and rattles off a bunch of random information for the record including that Piper is representing me and Trent is representing himself. Then the judge asks Piper what she has to present.

"Mr. Novak specifically requested at the time their relationship began that he and my client keep their finances separate and never mingle them," she begins. "The parties divided their rent for the entirety of their relationship up until the day they moved to New York—at which time my client contracted a lease on their penthouse apartment and paid the rent in her own name. Mr. Novak also specifically requested the pre-nuptial agreement currently lodged in the record. He had this agreement drawn up independently and presented it to my client prior to their wedding. The agreement specifically states that alimony and other post-marital compensation is disallowed. This was Mr. Novak's explicit request and we ask that the court uphold his wishes in this matter. All of his and my client's finances are already separated and have never co-mingled since they first met. My client supported Mr. Novak financially for a total of seven days after they moved to New York before he terminated their relationship and proceeded to enjoy himself with other women as though their marriage really was over. Let the record also reflect that my client earned her wealth through her own ingenuity and effort, that all of SigmaTech's original patents were developed and taken out under her name with no input, help, or financial contribution from Mr. Novak, and that he didn't even offer her encouragement to pursue this project in its inception. He continued to insist that she give it up even when the company became successful and she earned the rewards of her labors. Let the record reflect that Mr. Novak took no part in developing SigmaTech or its products or infrastructure. Our position is that Mr. Novak is entitled to no compensation, alimony, or other compensatory claims against my client's assets. We request that the marriage be dissolved without further complication and the parties go their separate ways with their own assets."

The judge turns to Trent. I can't stop my heart from pounding. This is the moment of truth.

"You may proceed with your case, Mr. Novak," the judge tells him. "Can you present any evidence to support your claim that Mrs. Novak was unfaithful to you during your marriage?"

Trent refuses to look up. He mumbles, "No, Your Honor."

"Can you present any justifiable cause why I should waive the alimony clause in the pre-nuptial agreement you went to such lengths to create?"

"No, Your Honor," Trent replies.

"And can you offer any evidence at all that you participated or even supported Mrs. Novak in building this company—or that you can lay any claim to her assets?"

"No, Your Honor."

The judge raises his eyebrows. "Then it is my ruling that the pre-nuptial agreement is valid and Mr. Novak is not entitled to any compensation, claim, or alimony in relation to Mrs. Novak. Let the record reflect that the marriage was dissolved this date the 17th of October and that the parties' assets and finances remain separated now as before without co-mingling. You are both free to remarry whenever you wish. Court is adjourned.

He bangs his gavel and calls the next case. I turn to Piper bursting with joy and excitement. I give her a huge hug. "Thank you so much!

You were brilliant! You were worth every penny! You can tell your husband I said so."

She laughs and beams at me. "Congratulations. Don't go spend it all in one place."

She has to pull me out of the way so the parties to the next hearing can move to the front of the courtroom. We talk all the way out of the building and I give her another hug on the sidewalk.

"I wish I could do something to thank you," I tell her. "I feel like I should be buying you a present or something."

"That's what the money is for, sweetie." She pushes me away and turns to get into a cab. "I'll see you around. Congratulations again, by the way—and don't do anything stupid tonight to celebrate, okay? Be smart and take your time."

I raise my hand to wave at her, and right then, Trent comes up to me from behind. "Paige?" he asks.

I turn around and all my happy excitement and relief goes right out the window when I come face to face with the scumbag. "What do you want?" I snap. "It's over. I hope you're happy. You could have ridden my meal ticket all the way to the bank, but you were too stupid even for that."

"I know...." He mumbles in hangdog pathetic misery. "I know...I just want to tell you....I'm leaving New York. I'm flying back home where I belong. I won't be around to bother you anymore. I thought I should tell you. Moving to New York was a bad idea...for me, at least. I can see it was the right thing for you, so I'll just leave and you can keep doing what you're doing."

My fury toward him dies. I want to tell him to get the hell out of my life forever—and that's exactly what he's doing.

I keep my voice steady—because I feel absolutely nothing for him. He's a stranger to me now. I don't even care that Piper is standing there listening to all of this.

"I think that's a good idea, Trent," I tell him. "I think that's the best thing for both of us. Let's part on civil terms and put this behind us."

He only nods and says, "See ya," before he walks off.

I watch him go. I didn't expect it to end like that, but I sure am glad he didn't turn it into another Piper-and-Judah situation.

He doesn't look back. He walks to the nearest subway station and disappears down the stairs. I take a minute before I turn around and face Piper.

"Are you okay?" she asks.

"Yeah!" I have to catch my breath and shake myself. "I wasn't expecting that."

"It sounds like he's ready to let bygones be bygones. You should do the same thing. I'll see you around sometime."

She gets into her cab, shuts the door, smiles at me through the window, and waves before the cab drives off. I take a few more minutes just to think about my life. I'm divorced. It's over. I'm free.

I set off walking across town. I could call a limo or flag a cab, but I want to take some time to just walk. This is just me without all the money and success and everything. I'm the same person I was before I founded SigmaTech.

I'm the same person I was before I ever met Trent. I'm just a girl from a small town in North Carolina. I'm nothing special. No one knows me. No one cares what I do. No tabloids are reporting on my personal life. I'm not rubbing elbows with billionaires and their wives.

I go home to my apartment. It's all mine now. New York is all mine. I don't have to worry about running into Trent or him making a stink about what I do. I can make my own decisions.

I decide to go out and celebrate just by myself. I need to take myself on a date and just enjoy my own company for the first time in years. I don't need another man. I don't need anything except to enjoy myself.

I won't do anything stupid. Piper is right about that. I don't want to throw my life away just when I got it back.

Chapter 14: Paige

I dress up in one of my nicest dresses, do my hair and makeup, and put on my nicest jewelry. I make a reservation for one in a fancy, expensive restaurant and call a limo to drive me.

I start to smile on my way there. Tonight is all about me. I don't need anyone to know me or acknowledge that tonight is such a special night for me. I feel happier than I've felt in years. I didn't realize Trent was dragging me down so much, but he obviously was.

I waltz into the restaurant and feel the eyes of men following me to my table. Are they wondering if I'm meeting a dashing, handsome date here?

Are they wondering if my date will be one of the wealthy, powerful men who commands this city and holds the reins of enterprise and influence?

I feel how hot and magnetic I look when I slide into a private booth by myself. I order myself a bottle of wine. The waiter pays extra special attention to me when he sees me alone. He makes deep eye contact with me while he pours my glass for me.

I give him my best smile and thank him warmly. He smiles back at me. He eats up my attention just like I eat up his. I'm a catch, I know it. He knows it. Every man in the room knows it.

I take my time drinking my wine and deciding what to order. I gaze out the window at the lights of New York. This city is mine to make it my own. I'm going to seize this city by the balls. I won't let anyone stop me ever again.

Piper is right about another thing. I need a man who is on my level if I get with anyone at all. I don't want to settle for someone who doesn't understand my world. I need someone who plays in the same ballpark and moves in the same circles.

I need someone who understands how important it is that I drive my company to the top. I need someone who encourages me instead of constantly coming up with reasons to hold me back.

I savor each bite of my meal. It's one of the most delicious meals I've ever eaten. Each bite floods my senses with exquisite pleasure because this is all mine. No one can take this moment away from me.

I stroll out of the restaurant afterward. I feel great. I feel ten feet tall and bulletproof.

I could call the limo to drive me, but I decide to go down to Broadway just because. I don't plan to see a show—not tonight. I just want to see the lights and feel the vibe.

I cruise down the sidewalk smiling at all the people in fancy clothes, a few in costumes, and other just normal people lining up to buy tickets for tonight's shows.

Some of the venues are tiny, hole-in-the-wall theaters that look more like shadowy dives than Broadway theaters. Some of the biggest Hollywood celebrity names flash in lights above the larger houses.

I can't wait to explore all of this, but tonight isn't about that. It's just about me.....and New York....alone at last. I absolutely freakin' love this town. Moving here is going to be the best thing that has ever happened to me.

I make it halfway up Broadway. I can already see the line of theaters fading into normal buildings beyond. I'm about to reenter the normal part of town. I would have to turn back to go into that world a second time.

I'm not ready to do that. I'll just go home after this.

Right then, a bunch of people come out of one of the nearby playhouses. This isn't a giant musical hall, but it isn't a dive, either.

It's a medium-sized theatrical venue and these people are obviously members of the cast. Some of them haven't removed all the makeup from around their eyes.

They flood the sidewalk around me and talk fast about going to the afterparty at a certain hotel back down the other end of Broadway. All of these people smile excitedly and their eyes sparkle with fun and excitement.

Then a bunch of the technical crew comes out in their black jeans, black T-shirts, and some of them are even still wearing their headsets.

They talk to the cast about the afterparty, who's bringing what, and what certain people still need to bring. Some of the crewmembers have to go back inside the theater to continue breaking the set for the night before they can leave.

The energy in front of the venue infects me with excitement. I follow the cast members down the street and a few of them ask me who I am and if I was in the audience. I tell them no, I was just standing there when they came out.

None of them tells me I'm not welcome to join them. They're all too high on life to care.

We flood into the hotel. The afterparty is happening in one of the downstairs lobby bars. Seventy people already pack the place and it becomes obvious that these people really did see the show.

They crowd around the cast members and everyone starts talking about the show, their characters, and random technical malfunctions no one in the audience noticed at the time.

Some of the guests are relatives of the cast and crew who came along to see their loved ones perform.

I get lost in the crowd. A lot of people come and talk to me. Our conversation shifts—and then a DJ starts playing dance music. Half the people in the bar start dancing. The others stand around talking, drinking, joking, and hugging each other.

Things get wild when the crew shows up and everyone lets their hair down. I move through the crowd talking to anyone and everyone. This is fantastic.

I get to know a bunch of the cast and crew. They're all super nice and super committed to their craft. They think their work is the greatest thing since sliced bread—and I can't really argue with that.

A few different guys ask me to dance and I go with them. I let loose on the dance floor, but everyone acts very respectful. None of the guys come onto me more than to ask me to dance.

Two different guys put their hands on my hips while I dance. I don't try to stop them and they don't try to touch me any more than that. They make me feel sexy and alive. They make me feel appealing and attractive even though I'm now officially divorced.

I leave the dance floor to go back to the bar. I have to elbow my way through the crowd and get waylaid talking to different people.

Random strangers who weren't involved in the show or in the audience start to filter in. It becomes less of an afterparty for the cast and crew and more just a regular party. I love it.

I'm just making my way to the bar when I spot Kevin standing at one of the nearby tables. It's a tall drinking table with no stools around it. He's standing there talking to two other men in suits while they both sip their drinks.

His eyes widen when he sees me. I wave and walk past him to get a glass of soda from the bar. I don't want to drink anything alcoholic—not now.

I'm just pulling my credit card out of a secret pocket of my dress to pay the bartender when Kevin leaves his table and comes up to me. "You are the last person I expected to see at a place like this," he tells me.

I grin up at him and sip my soda through a straw while I wait for the bartender to run my card through the till.

"I'm celebrating my divorce. We just finalized it at the courthouse a few hours ago and Trent is leaving town to go home to North Carolina. So I took myself out on a date tonight and now I'm enjoying myself at a party." I glance behind him. "Please tell me you weren't conducting business just now."

He laughs and his cheeks color. "I can't help it. I can't show my face in public without seeing someone I know and they all want to talk to me. It isn't my fault I'm one of the popular kids in school."

I snicker at his joke and take my card back from the bartender. Some other guys come off the dance floor just then and jostle me trying to get to the bar.

Kevin puts his arm behind my back to steer me back to the table his counterparts just vacated.

I try not to notice that he's putting his arm behind me—and then his hand comes to rest right on my spine. He really is touching me like that and treating me like we're here together as a couple.

Chapter 15: Paige

I stop at the table to sip my drink through my straw. Kevin pivots around the other side of the table and stands opposite me.

Now I can see the look in his eyes—and he is definitely looking at me like that. I know exactly what he's thinking and it isn't platonic. Not by a mile.

"Do you mind if I join you in your date for one?" he asks.

"Not at all. I'm delighted to see you here."

"How did the hearing go?"

"Oh, it went absolutely smashingly. Piper is a genius. She really is. She absolutely smoked Trent. He represented himself—except that he didn't represent himself. He agreed to all our terms and didn't try to fight the pre-nup. He agreed that he contributed nothing to SigmaTech's success, that we kept our finances separate through our whole relationship because that was his wish, that he was the one who asked for a pre-nup and drew it up with a no-alimony clause, and that I hadn't supported him financially before we moved to New York. He offered no argument or objection. He just accepted the ruling and told me he was leaving town. I was really dreading it turning into another violent nightmare like Judah and Piper had to go through, but it went surprisingly well. Hiring her was the best decision I ever made."

"Wow. Congratulations. So what's next for you?"

"Nothing too flashy. I'm just going to work on building a life here, seeing all the sights, enjoying everything New York has to offer, and settling in the way I should have to begin with. I love my new apartment. I love my job. I love everything about being here. I'm so happy I moved here—and I love the club. I couldn't be happier that I can finally join. That's one of the greatest perks of all of this."

He beams at me. "It's great that you could finally join. It was such a disappointment when Trent told you not to."

I can't help but smile at him. "You and the other billionaires have been so nice. I'm really sorry I turned it into something I shouldn't have. That was a mistake. I never should have crossed that line."

He doesn't say anything. He doesn't tell me it was nothing nor does he tell me that he's glad I kissed him. It doesn't matter now because we aren't going there.

I try to change the subject. "Anyway, what about you? What brings you out tonight?"

He shrugs. "I was supposed to meet someone at a bar down the block, but they didn't show up, so another person I happen to know invited me to come here. It just worked out that way."

I cock my head to study him. "You say that like the person you were supposed to meet was a date or something."

"No, no, nothing like that. A young man call up the People, Inc. office the other day. He said he has an engineering degree and wants us to place him in a position using his qualification, but he's working in this other bar and couldn't make it into the office to meet with any of us. So I said I would come down and meet him on his break—which was at seven-thirty tonight—but the manager said the guy quit last week—which was before he called the office. So the kid was obviously telling us a line of crap about the whole thing. I still don't know why he did it."

"So you came all the way down here to interview some kid for a job placement? Don't you have other people to do that for you?"

He shrugs. "I like to keep track of my people. I don't have anyone specifically assigned for situations like this and it helps the company if I get personally involved with everyone's situations. If someone needs help, then they usually need help from me, not some flunky I sent out to do my dirty work because I'm too up my own ass to do it myself."

I laugh. "You really are something else, Kevin. You know that?"

"Why? I like to take care of people—especially people who put their faith in me and my company. If this kid had been sincere and had been telling the truth about who he was and his circumstances, then People, Inc. would have been the perfect organization to get him out of all of this and get him into a role where he would be able to thrive. That's what we do. If that means I have to come down here to talk to him in person, then I consider it a small price to pay for such a vast benefit it would make to that young man's life. How could I reasonably turn my back on that? I don't see how any sane person could leave another human being in the lurch like that."

I stare back at him. He really is something exceptional—and he doesn't even realize it. He thinks this is all normal.

He sees me staring at him and shoots a glance toward the dance floor before he comes back to looking at me. "Is something wrong?" he asks.

"No, not at all. I admire you. You're doing great work. I'm impressed." I take another sip of my drink.

"Would you like to go over there on the other side of the room where we'll be farther away from the DJ?" he asks. "It won't be as loud over there."

"Okay, sure." We start migrating through the crowd to the other side of the bar. He's right that the speakers are all on this side of the room. It's a lot louder over here.

We get to the other side of the room and I put my glass on another standing drink table, but he doesn't take a position on the other side. He comes toward me. The smoldering look in his eyes and the energy vibrating off his body is overpowering.

He comes right up to me, stands right in front of me, and stares down deep into my eyes from directly above. He's four or five inches taller than me and feels much bigger all of a sudden.

I don't know what changed for him—except that I'm divorced now. It definitely changed. The charge of tension electrifies me and instantly turns me on. He's coming onto me—strong.

He starts to dance in a slow, undulating, side-to-side movement that eases his body closer to me if that's even possible. He hovers right in front of my eyes—close enough to kiss me—but he doesn't kiss me.

He sways there brooding like he really wants to kiss me—and do so much more to me. His movements infect me with such a powerful, sexual, hypnotic sense that he's already doing it to me. He would look at me like this if he did it with me.

I start dancing with him and match his movements. My body responds to him out of all proportion. He's unbelievably hot like this—and he wants me. That's what this means.

He kept himself on a leash before—except that he wasn't even thinking about that before tonight. I'm certain he wasn't. My divorce must have given him permission to finally recognize the chemistry between us.

I can't tear my eyes away from that mesmerizing gaze. He never shows this side of himself during his business day. He always behaves with perfect professional decorum at all times.

That man is nowhere in sight. He completely discards it and another side of him comes out of hiding. This man is volcanic, powerful, and unbelievably sexually ravenous. He sees what he wants and never wavers until he hunts it down.

He keeps moving toward me and easing me back until he pushes me against the wall. He doesn't touch me even then. He leaves just a few maddening inches between his body and mine.

He buzzes with so much unbridled passion right there underneath his clothes. I can't stand the tension any longer. I raise my hand and wind up touching his chest right at the angle of his sternum. His muscles tense under his shirt.

He still doesn't move toward me at all—not right away. He stands there spiraling back and forth. He has a slow, sultry, almost catlike way of dancing. It looks smooth and alluring even though he doesn't dance as fast as everyone else in the room.

He raises his arms and places them on the wall above my head. He stays there shadowing me from the rest of the room. His bulk hides me and everything else he's doing to me—even though he isn't doing anything to me.

My body bursts into flame from the way he's looking at me and moving nearer and more suggestively all the time. I run my hand down his stomach. He feels tight and chiseled and muscular under there, but his suit hides it in daylight.

I grab his belt, pull him the rest of the way toward me, and raise my face to kiss him just as he bends down to kiss me. Our lips meet in a torrent of pure, scorching, unchained passion unlike anything I've ever felt.

He keeps his arms planted above my head and his body keeps making those slow, brutal, provocative waves up and down my stomach and thighs while his mouth consumes all that I am.

He leans all his weight against me and grinds into me with mind-blowing power. His lips and tongue wring the agonized moans of deepest craving from my very soul. No one has ever kissed me like this.

He fights for breath through his nostrils each time our heads turn sideways to open our mouths. I can't stop touching him all over his chest, stomach, and sides under his jacket.

He doesn't stop me from touching him. He stays in the same position grinding his body against me and driving himself hard as a rock.

He doesn't try to hide his prick throbbing against me through his clothes. He flexes his knees and straightens them to thrust up into me.

His mouth devours my mind. I claw at his shirt in mindless hunger. I need him. I want him. Everything about him attracts me like no one else I've ever met.

I admire him. He's the sweetest, most caring man I've ever met. I've never even heard of anyone doing something like he tried to do tonight. He gave up his personal time to travel across town on the slim chance that he could help someone he'd never even met.

I know enough about him and his character. Spending the night with him or even casually hooking up with him—it wouldn't be stupid—not at all. It would be wonderful.

I can't think of any man I would rather get involved with even casually. Whatever we do—kissing right now or even going all the way—it won't ruin our working relationship.

He wouldn't be doing this right now if he thought it would. He might even be making the first move because he thinks there's a chance we could work out as a couple. I can't think of anything better than that.

He's so unbelievably hot. Kissing him drives me wild. I want him right now this very minute.

Chapter 16: Paige

Kevin eases away from me first. It isn't like I can ease off when I have my back pinned against the wall.

He doesn't stand up straight—not yet. He stays where he is, stops kissing me, and glares down at me with that haunted, hungry, smoldering look of his while he keeps grinding his body against me.

Watching him almost makes me climax just from how hot he is right now.

My hand rises automatically without any conscious thought on my part. I trail my fingertips down his lips and they fall open to reveal his bared teeth inside his mouth. I want that mouth. I want his body and all that he is. He's intoxicating like this.

He responds by taking one of his arms down from the wall. He uses the other to keep himself propped there in the same position.

His weight and slow grinding movements tell me exactly what it would feel like if we were doing it right now. My mind shuts down in the torched, insatiable desire for him.

I stare up into his eyes and let him see me pant and shudder with every delirious pulse of his body against mine. I want him to tear my clothes off and ravage me right here in public. But he won't do that.

He clasps his free hand around my jaw and holds my face there where he can see me trembling for him. He dives in, snatches one kiss, and pulls back just enough to see my face right there in his hand. He can do what he wants with me when he looks at me like this.

He does it once more, steals one more molten kiss, straightens up, takes his other hand down, and turns away toward the table. He turns his back to me and stands there with his head bowed while he studies his drink in his hand.

I don't know what to think of his reaction. Is that it? Does he regret kissing me?

I walk over to the table and make sure to leave a safe distance between us while I pick up my drink and take a sip.

He looks up at me and our eyes meet. He looks as tortured and haunted now as he did a minute ago except that he doesn't let his predatory sexual side show in front of the world.

Does he ever show it to anyone? Am I the only person alive who has ever seen him like that?

His eyes lock on me with unbelievable power. He doesn't look away. His expression overflows with longing, fury, frustration, and guarded resignation that he'll never get what he wants in that way.

"Do you need a ride home?" he finally asks. "I can drive you in my car if you don't want to walk. It's getting awfully late for a lady dressed like that to be walking down the street alone."

I have to smile at him. "That's really nice of you. I would appreciate that."

His eyes shoot down to my dress and body. "You look incredible, by the way. You always do, but that....." He forces himself to look away.

"Why are you single?" I blurt out. "I mean....are you single? Are you seeing anyone? Why aren't you married like all the other guys? I would have thought some lucky girl would come along and snagged you."

"I don't know. I guess I just belong to anyone and everyone. People are my thing. I've never focused on one person before."

"So....have you ever dated anyone? Are you seriously telling me you don't have a woman in your life? I'm stunned."

"I have dated before—not for a long time. It always winds up all over the news when one of the guys in the club starts dating any-one—or one of the girls in the club starts dating anyone. It all goes out there on public display. I didn't want that—not unless it was going to be serious—and it never is. The girls who express interest in us aren't serious about anything. It couldn't be more obvious that they're anything but serious."

"So you can't find anyone serious? I bet you could if you tried."

"I guess that's kinda the point. I don't try. I don't think about it—and I don't sleep around. My reputation is more important to me. My reputation is my company's reputation, so it's important that I behave a certain way in public."

"So......what is it that we just did over there? Are we going to go back to pretending it never happened?"

He gulps and his eyes go hard. "I don't want to pretend it never happened."

"What do you want to happen?"

"Do you really want to know? I want to put you in my limo and take you home with me. That's what I want."

I blink at him. "You do? Are you sure?"

He snorts. "Are you kidding me? Did I not make it clear enough just now—because I can do it again....and again....and again.....until you get the message."

I turn bright red and look away. "You don't have to do that. I got the message. You just made it clear the other day that you didn't want t o."

"I wanted to then, too—but you're divorced now—and I didn't want to overstep my position as membership officer by moving in on you during the application process. That wouldn't have been appropriate."

"Is there a rule against officers and members getting together with each other?"

"No, there isn't a rule against it. Any of the members can get together with each other whenever they want to."

"Is there some kind of waiting period between when a member joins and when an existing member can express interest?"

"No, it isn't like that. It's just my thing. I don't want anyone to think I'm using my position to pick out the ripest, juiciest prospects the minute they walk through the door. I don't want to think of myself that way, either."

I burst out laughing. "Thank you for the compliment."

"You're welcome. I was referring to you."

I blush and lower my eyes. "Thank you, Kevin. I got that—but something tells me the prospects that walk through the door don't interest you in that way. Something tells me you don't respond to them the way you responded to me."

"Of course I don't. They're all men, and the very few times we get women, they don't appeal to me. I'm happy when they join, but being membership officer isn't about that—just like it wasn't about that with you. You mentioned that you were married and that was the end of it. I still thought you were dynamite, though."

I can't stop smiling at him. "I thought that about you, too—and I still do."

He stares at me for a second before he grabs my hand. He pulls me through the crowd and back out onto the street. I don't see until I get there that he has his phone out.

He glances up and down Broadway. It's much quieter now. Most of the shows have already finished and the crowds have gone home.

He sets off leading me by the hand up the sidewalk. I hurry to keep up with him. I don't know where we're going—except that he said he wants to take me home with him.

Chapter 17: Paige

Kevin and I make it as far as the nearest corner before a long, sleek black limo pulls up Broadway behind us. It angles in at the curb at the corner. Kevin opens the rear passenger door for me to get in and he climbs in behind me.

He slams the door and the car glides away into the night. Kevin barely sits down on the seat before he turns around and pulls me toward me kissing me just as deeply and intensely as he did in the bar.

He scoops one arm behind my back and wraps his other hand around my thigh to turn me toward him. I can't spread my legs with this dress holding my thighs together.

His kiss lights me on fire all over again. He tips me backward and I drape my arms around his neck. "Come home with me," he whispers in the darkness.

I gasp in a ragged panting breath, but I can't speak. His hands start to crawl all over me the way I touched him in the bar.

He scoops up my sides and grips my ribs right below my breasts. His fingers give just a hint of suggestion of what he might do if he let himself do it.

His breath burns my lips and cheeks. I crave him. I need him to touch me. I need him to consume me and show me all the boiling hot fire hidden in his soul. I need this with him just for one night before he goes back to being perfectly professional.

His hands slither down my sides, around my back, to my hip, and back to my outer thigh. He doesn't touch me any more than that. He never ventures into any uncharted or forbidden territory.

I want to climb on top of him and for him to climb on top of me. I want him to ravage me right here in the limo. Kissing him like this turns me on beyond belief. I can't stand to wait.

Just thinking that seems to set him off. He slides his hand a little farther down my thigh to my bare knee. He grips it once and slips his hand between my thighs to crush my leg on the inside this time.

I moan and whine in an agony of desire—and like magic, he pulls off my mouth and glares down at me with that fuming, predatory look he gave me in the club.

Streetlights flash past the limo windows from outside. The light barely casts his face in a white glow before he plunges back into darkness. The distant lights of stores and windows reflect off the glassy surface of his eyes staring down at me.

I pant and sob in a combination of brutal pleasure and aching, throbbing hot desire for more. I want him to slide his hand the rest of the way up between my legs and rub and finger me to make me climax.

I want to ride his hand and let him see me shake and convulse for him. I want him to make me scream and for him to savor the sound of my tormented moans as I cry out for him.

His eyes tell me that's exactly what he wants. He's taking me home so he can do all of that to me. I need him so damn bad I can't stand it.

He creeps his hand up just a little higher and squeezes again—just enough to make me writhe on the seat in front of him. His hard, unforgiving eyes never leave my face. He watches every quiver and grimace.

He knows he's doing this to me. He knows he's turning me on and reducing me to a desperate, wretched, hungry mess. Will he ever take it further? Will he ever finish me off?

He draws his hand away all too soon and leaves me whimpering and moaning for more of his touch. He pulls my arm down from his neck and steers my hand by the wrist to touch him between his legs.

He places my hand right on top of his straining, rigid shaft. He spasms and his cheek jolts when I touch him through the fabric of his pants.

He doesn't break eye contact and I don't, either. I stare up into those voracious, ravenous eyes while I stroke him harder and faster. He glares at me and his lips curl back from his teeth to snarl at me. His power melts my insides when he looks at me like that.

I grip him tighter and stroke him in a steady, escalating rhythm. Will he let me bring him to his own release right now? Something tells me he won't.

He doesn't. He just stays there watching me stroke him until the limo pulls into some kind of covered structure in a side street somewhere. I don't realize until we get there that we're inside a ground-level garage big enough to house the limo.

Fluorescent lights flicker on overhead and a motorized lever door pivots down behind us to enclose the garage from the street outside.

The garage is totally empty except for the limo. Carpet covers the concrete floor and the walls have been tastefully sheet-rocked and painted the same as the interior walls of a house.

The driver doesn't get out of the limo. The window between the driver's compartment and the passenger compartment stays closed the whole time. I never see the driver's face even once.

Kevin opens the door, gets out first, and holds out his hand to help me get out of the car. He crosses to a door in the wall and opens it to reveal an elevator behind it.

The elevator only has one button. He presses it and holds the door open until the elevator opens in front of us. He keeps his hold on my hand while I step inside and he follows me.

The outer, normal-looking door swings shut just as the elevator doors slide together to close us in. Kevin keeps holding my hand on the way up into the building. He casts occasional glances at me every now and then, but he doesn't talk.

What is he thinking right now? Does he think he's about to do something he'll later regret? I don't want him to think that. I want him to enjoy tonight. I want him to look forward to it and look back on it with good memories.

I don't break the silence. I won't regret tonight no matter what happens. I don't even care if this is just a casual hookup for him. I respect him too much to regret doing anything with him.

The elevator doesn't have any interior buttons for him to press to tell it where to take us. I guess this elevator only goes one place.

I find out why when it stops at the top. It opens into a gigantic penthouse much bigger than anything I've seen before.

The elevator opens into one of several living areas. The penthouse covers the whole floor of the building in one big open sprawling extravaganza of luxury.

Windows surround us on all sides. Indoor trees, shelves, screens, furniture, and other tasteful furnishings separate each living area from the others. Each one has its own unique vibe, décor, and amusements.

One of them has a big granite wall in the middle of the apartment with a flat, modern, artistic fireplace in it. The living area on the opposite side of this wall has a flatscreen TV big enough to double as a home theater. Couches surround both the TV and the fireplace.

Each living area appeals to me in a different way. Each one breathes comfort and relaxation without sacrificing luxury and expensive taste.

Kevin turns aside and puts his phone on one of the end tables next to a couch. He doesn't interfere while I wander from one exquisite sight to the next.

This apartment is unlike anything I ever thought possible—and yet it's all so uniquely him. His personality comes through in every detail.

This apartment feels like he must have picked out every piece of furniture, every plant, and every painting on the wall to make it as welcoming as possible to any visitors who stop by. The apartment is a living space first and foremost. It's beyond welcoming.

A deco glass staircase leads down to the next floor of the building with a pool, kitchen and dining area, and what looks like a recreational area with an indoor tennis court, racquetball court, weight room, and another area with a whole bunch of different exercise equipment.

Another identical staircase rises to the upper floor. A bunch of interior walls block me from seeing anything up there. All the bedrooms must be up there.

Subtle, tasteful area lights brighten the apartment from the high ceiling. They don't make the apartment too bright or too dim. They give just enough light to make it relaxing. It's nighttime, so the light is lower than it would be during the day.

I stop at one of the windows looking out. The apartment doesn't have an outdoor terrace or anything like that. The apartment extends right to the edge of the building's vertical walls.

"This place is incredible," I exclaim.

"I spend a lot of time here," he replies from across the room. "I want it to be a nice place I enjoy spending time."

"It's more than nice. It's magnificent—and yet so relaxing. I don't feel like I'm stepping into a castle where I'm afraid to touch anything or sit on any of the furniture. Everything feels so warm and hospitable."

I don't say, *Like you, Kevin*, but I'm thinking it. Of course his home would be the same way. It's a reflection of him.

"Do you think so?" he asks. "I want it to be that way."

"Do you get many visitors?"

He looks away. "You are actually the first visitor I've had here."

I spin around. "What?! Why?"

He shrugs. "I don't know. It just never worked out that way, I guess. The other club members sometimes invite us all over to their places for various occasions. I could do the same thing here, but we're always going somewhere or other. We either see each other at club events or we meet in town for business dinners or lunches or someone invites everyone over to their place. I guess I just never got around to it. We all see so much of each other. It's the same with people at work. We see each other all the time. It isn't like we need to see each other any other time. We have regular company parties and activity days together, but we usually hold those on the company recreation floor or at another venue that's big enough for everyone. I had no reason to invite them here."

"Does your family ever come to visit you?"

He snorts. "Hell no. They would never do that."

"Why not? Are they ashamed of you?"

"Quite the contrary. They're extremely proud of me."

"I bet. They should be."

"I go up there to visit them. My grandparents are too old to travel—and it's always understood that any far-flung relatives who want to visit will go back there to do it. I go home for Christmas, Thanksgiving, Easter, and a few other holidays every year. That's the rule. We go there. Everyone goes there."

"Do you have far-flung relatives in other parts of the country?"

He crosses the apartment to a different living area. They're all interconnected enough that we can talk easily from one to another. I stand in the one with the fireplace. He crosses to a more open area with couches, a coffee table, and a few wing-backed chairs near one of the outer windows.

He waves at what looks like a long, narrow dresser between this outer sitting area and the rest of the apartment. "Do you want anything to drink?" he asks. "We have non-alcoholic stuff."

"We?" I tease. "Who's we?"

"You and me." He bends down and opens one of the cupboards under the dresser. The cupboard opens into a hidden drinks fridge. "I have soda, carbonated water, and juice."

"I'm fine, thank you. I don't need anything."

He shuts the fridge and sits down on a different couch. He looks and acts perfectly relaxed here in his own personal habitat. He doesn't act like me being here puts him at all on edge or that he's doing anything out of the ordinary by bringing his first visitor home.

He also doesn't draw attention to the fact that the first visitor he's ever brought home is a woman he picked up at a bar. He doesn't act like we made out at the bar or in the limo on the way here. He doesn't act like I ever touched him in such an explicitly sexual way.

Chapter 18: Paige

I copy Kevin by sitting down on the couch in front of the fireplace. This feels like an especially cozy place someone might want to curl up on a cold winter night.

"I have a few cousins and siblings living in different parts of the country and different parts of the world," he tells me in answer to my question. "They're all married and raising their own children. They all go home to Boston and we see each other there. They have no interest in coming here. My way of life doesn't appeal to them. They don't understand it. They've all come to accept that this is the way I do things, but they don't share it and they don't want to see enough of it to understand it."

"That's....I guess I can't say it's sad. It's just different."

"Is it? Is it different for you? What do your relatives think about the direction your career has gone? Do they understand and accept it?"

Now it's my turn to snort and look away. "They do neither. They don't understand it. They don't accept it. They consider it an unforgivable betrayal that I succeeded and became wealthy. They act like I sold my soul to the devil and became some other species of grotesque evil fiend for trying to help people and actually making some money at it."

He lowers his voice. "I'm sorry that happened to you. You aren't the first member of the club to go through that."

"I had a few of my best friends—women I had been friends with all the way through grade school, high school, and college—they actually disowned me and told me they never wanted to see or hear from me again because I offered to use my money to help them out financially. One of their teenage daughters needed emergency dental surgery to fix an abscessed tooth. I offered to pay for the surgery because I knew my friend and her husband couldn't afford it. The woman completely went off on me, called me a bunch of terrible names, told me I had betrayed our friendship, and threatened to call the Police if I ever contacted her, talked to any of her family again, or even looked at her in public. She and her husband took out a high-interest home equity loan on their house to pay for the surgery. The loan hiked up their mortgage payments beyond what they could afford to pay and they wound up losing their house. They had to rent after that."

"Wow," he breathes. "That's awful."

"She wasn't the only one. My younger sister's eight-year-old son got diagnosed with the same condition as my younger brother. I offered to make arrangements for our local hospital to use my equipment to treat my nephew, but my sister refused and said she wouldn't take any charity from me. My nephew suffered in agony for over a year before he died—and then she blamed me for his death."

I can't hold back the tears. I've never talked to anyone about this. I never even told Trent. I've been carrying this secret around in my heart for years.

All the other slights and insults come out at the same time—all the pain of my brother's death, all of Trent's snide comments about me working too much and treating him badly because he didn't have my money—and then the hurt, humiliation, and betrayal of him sleeping around like that.

I cover my face with my hands and burst into tears right there in front of Kevin. I can't even care that he's seeing me like this. I needed to talk to someone about it—and he seems to be the best person.

That's his superpower. He accepts everyone no matter who they are and what terrible secrets they're hiding.

All the pain of those memories comes rushing to the surface. I realize in that moment that I feel safe with him. I can let him see me like this because.....well, because he's Kevin. I'm sure everyone who knows him unloads on him like this. He's the safest man alive.

He doesn't move from his couch. He sits there in silence watching me cry my heart out. I would be embarrassed to cry like this in front of anyone else, but I don't feel embarrassed in front of him. It's okay because I trust him completely.

He waits a long time for me to stop. He doesn't come over to me until after I stop crying and straighten up on my own. I take my hands down and wipe the tears off my cheeks. I'm sure I look like a nightmare now.

He stands up, takes a box of tissues off a different side table, and brings it over to me.

I thank him in a husky undertone when I take it from him, blow my nose, and wipe the mascara off my cheeks. I open my bag and check in my compact mirror so I don't look too hideous.

He stands there waiting in silence until I finish. I finally ball up the tissue and put it and the mirror in my purse. I'll throw the tissue away later.

He doesn't give me a chance to look up at him. He cups my cheeks in both hands and lifts my face to so he can see me. He gazes down at me with a mixed expression. A hundred emotions war in his face, but he always looks like he admires me and cares for me.

He strokes his thumbs down my cheeks and pets my swollen face. He uses his fingertips to comb the hair off my forehead and traces the line of my eyebrows, down my cheek, and goes back to holding my face oh, so gently.

I see so many shades of him when he looks at me like this. He's the collected executive steering the lives of thousands or maybe even millions of people. He's the smoldering predator from the bar. He's the sweet, kind friend who takes care of everyone.

I know I'm as special to him as he is to me. He cares for me the same way he cares for everyone else, but he feels differently about me. I'm in another category for him. I must be if he brought me home like this. He doesn't bring anyone else home.

He finally lowers himself onto his knees in front of me, rests his hands on the couch cushion on either side of my hips, and kneels there to kiss me.

We both sink into that kiss as effortless as it was before. There's no friction or awkwardness. Kissing him feels like we've been doing it this way all our lives the same way I felt like I had known him and been doing business with him all our lives.

I wrap my arms around his neck and vanish in the dark bliss of warmth coming from his lips. His tongue sizzles with pure luscious energy in my mouth, but it also overflows my being with warmth, comfort, safety, and acceptance.

His hands make their usual migration over my body the way they did in the car. He follows my sides down to my hips, up my back—and I freeze when he takes hold of the zipper in the back of my dress.

He doesn't stop kissing me—not ever—not even when my eyes fly open in sudden realization of what he's doing.

He stares at me from just beyond my nose. His lips keep moving with mine while he glides my zipper down. The tightness of my dress around me loosens and starts to fall away.

He pulls off my mouth and straightens up to stare down at me. His eyes ask a million questions. Am I really going to go through with this? Will I suddenly change my mind and decide I don't like him or trust him enough for that?

He kneels in front of me holding me spellbound with those eyes while he moves his hands to my knees. The same charge of lightning rushes up my thighs when he touches my bare skin.

He rakes his fingertips up my outer thighs and scratches my dress farther up so he can pull my legs apart. I sob in a wave of agonized desire when I see him like this. My lips pout with panting hunger at the look in his eyes. He's magnificent.

He scoots my dress up to my hips and squeezes deep, massaging handfuls up my thighs to make me ache for him.

My head spins from all the heat rushing through me from his hands and eyes. I touch his shirt again.....and my eyes dip to his tie. He's undressing me, so why not?

I look back up at him while I tug his tie loose and push his jacket off. He doesn't stop me. He keeps caressing my body and gripping my thighs while I unbutton his shirt—and then one hand clamps on my breast through my dress.

His features go hard and brutal watching me shudder and moan in front of his eyes. He keeps squeezing and pinching my breasts through my bra and dress while I unbutton his shirt. His power drives me out of my mind.

I can barely see anything in front of me by the time I open his shirt and my hand lands on his bare chest. He's beautifully lean underneath, but he isn't as big as some of the guys in the club. He has a long, athletic build that somehow makes him more appealing.

He doesn't respond to my touch—or he doesn't show that he responds. He focuses on me and my reaction. He lets go of my breasts, puts his arms behind me, and drags his fingers up the bare skin of my back where my zipper used to be.

That touch makes me whine and moan in front of him. I have to shut my eyes and lower my head trying to cope with the intensity that he's touching me like this.

The feeling that I trust him, that I'm safe with him—it all comes to a boiling point in that moment of undeniable need. He's the one I need. He's the one I ache for. He's everything I want.

He tugs the top straps of my dress forward and slips it down to expose my bra. He doesn't take my dress off any further than that nor does he touch my breasts or my bra at all.

He leans back and lets his appreciative eye trail all over me—all the parts he can see. He grips my knees, works his hot, strong hands up my thighs, and sinks his mouth into my thighs between my legs.

I can't stop moaning as he mouths his way higher toward my saturated panties. He keeps both hands clamped on my thighs to hold them apart like he needs to restrain me in place for his pleasure.

I squirm and writhe on the couch trying to survive the agonizing heat rushing up into my core to burn my flesh. He works back and forth from one thigh to the other electrifying all that sensitive skin with the heat and wetness of his mouth.

I need his mouth on me. I need his fingers inside me and his body taking me to the stars. I need all of that, but he keeps me trembling and longing for him with never any completion.

He hears me sobbing for it, but he still doesn't work high enough to get there. He stops just short of my panties.

I grab his head and try to pull him in, but he doesn't. He does as he pleases and teases me to the breaking point. I want to cry, I need him so bad.

He straightens up on his knees and towers over me watching me grimace and moan in front of his eyes. Did he want this? Did he want to see me like this all those weeks and months while we sat across from each other at the negotiating table?

I can't stand the way he's looking at me—like I'm a delicacy he's going to enjoy feasting on—but he can take his time and drag it out as long as possible to give himself the maximum possible pleasure.

Chapter 19: Paige

I sit up straight in front of Kevin. He still kneels between my spread legs. His shirt hangs open to reveal his chest.

He touches me the way he wants to. Now it's my turn. I lower my hand between his legs and stroke him the way I did in the car. He holds my eyes no matter what and watches my expression.

His face and body show no sign that I'm doing anything to him. He doesn't change his facial expression.

He doesn't shudder and quake the way he makes me shudder and quake, but his shaft spasms in my hand and throbs and jerks each time I pass my hand down its length. He feels masterful down there. I want to unzip him and get him to take it further—so much further.

He finally sits back on his ankles, takes my hands, and guides me to stand up in front of him. He stays kneeling while he slides my dress down my hips and legs to the floor. He doesn't take my shoes off.

He stays there below me and gazes up at me standing in my bra and panties. He caresses his hands all over my bare body—up my sides, squeezes my breasts through my bra, sweeps behind my back, grips my ass in two big handfuls, and massages down the backs of my thighs.

He gazes on me with heartfelt admiration and genuine appreciation of what he sees. His hands and eyes devour me in pure desire. He makes me feel so sexy and appealing—like he can't get enough of me. I don't want him to stop looking at me like that—not ever.

He would never be satisfied just to look and touch. He guides me back down on the couch, kisses me for another long, torturous moment, and then holds eye contact while he slides my panties down.

He holds them open for me to step out of, pushes my thighs apart, and works his mouth up them until he finally closes his hot lips on my sensitive, aching, quivering flesh.

I fall back on my elbows and let myself sink into the rapture of him teasing me and nagging me to the heights of glory. He grips my ass and pulls me into his mouth, flickers my clitoris until I scream, and lifts my thighs over his shoulders to position me where he wants me.

He strips off his shirt while he's down there. His muscles strain and bulge every time he does something with his arms to adjust my position.

I claw at his shoulders and try to grab his hair, but he's flooding me with so much pleasure that I can't stop him. He escalates one wave at a time, slips his fingers into me, and builds me up to a screaming climax.

I thrash and shriek as he tears me apart. He doesn't stop even then. I fall apart on the couch in front of him and struggle to contain all the explosions going off inside me.

He adjusts the pressure and softens his mouth so he doesn't push me too far. He takes bigger bites and eases everything off so he still teases me to raving madness without going past what I can tolerate.

I can't take this. He gives me so much pleasure and leaves me yearning for more, but he doesn't satisfy the deepest desire of my heart by letting me join with him.

He rises up to stand over me and stares down at me with all that smoldering passion. He doesn't take his fingers out of me.

He keeps gliding them in again and again, wringing the juicy succulent wetness from me to show how much I need him, and circles his soft fingers through my flesh to make me moan.

He watches every wave of bliss and agony crossing my face. Nothing escapes him—not how much I need him, not how much I feel for him, not how much my body trembles before his presence.

He sees me splayed out for his hands to explore. He doesn't stop until he's ready—and he doesn't stop even then. He pulls his hands out just for an instant—just enough time for me to realize he's going to do something.

He takes hold of one of my legs, pulls it across himself, and rolls me onto my stomach. My knees and thighs fall over the couch so I bend over in front of him with my bare ass and exposed, saturated flesh pointed toward him.

Now he'll take me. Now he'll slam into me and make me scream. I can't live another minute without feeling that he possesses me.

He doesn't, though, of course not. That would be too easy.

He lies across my back breathing heavily into my ear. His panting breaths match the rhythmic undulations of his rock-solid body against my back. His hardness grinds into my ass from behind and makes me moan again.

He scoops one hand under my jaw and pries my head back so he can hear me whine and roar for him. God, I need him to take me like this! I need him to conquer me and own me as his own. I need that beyond words.

He pulls away all too soon. He drives me insane when he teases me like this. He does a million things other than take me.

He lowers himself on his knees behind me, buries his face in me from behind, and devours me a second time in that position.

He burrows deep into my sodden flesh until I scream out in raging lust. His fingers drill me to the core until he explodes me into a million pieces.

He doesn't wait around anymore for me to come down. He stands up, scoops me into his arms, and walks off with me toward the stairs leading up to the bedrooms.

I collapse on his shoulder sobbing and moaning in desperate need. I need him to protect me and take care of me. That's what he's doing, but we aren't finished for the night. He's just getting started.

He stops somewhere along the way and punches a button on an electronic wall panel to turn the lights off downstairs. He carries me up the stairs, down a hallway, and into an enormous bedroom.

This one is set in another corner of the upper floor. The giant windows of the two outer walls come together in the corner showing the same majestic view of New York lying before us. Those lights shine into the bedroom enough for me to see the layout.

The massive bed sits on a raised platform to create the illusion that the rest of the room is a kind of private sunken living room with couches, chairs, and its own coffee table.

Another interior wall cuts off the opposite corner of the room to form a triangular closet behind the bed.

He climbs up, lays me on the bed, and lets me relax there while he sits next to me and strokes my body. I'm still struggling to contain all the power coursing through me.

He lights me up in ways I never thought possible. I want more of him. I want to share all the delights of his body and for him to share mine.

He caresses me for a while and watches me sigh and calm down on his bed. I'm in his room. This is where it happens. This is where we'll spend the night together.

He eventually turns aside to untie his shoes and kick them off. He left his shirt, tie, jacket, and my dress and panties downstairs. I guess we would have to go there to get them back.

He pushes his shoes aside, pivots around, and lies back on the bed with his head and shoulders propped against a big pile of pillows. He pulls me into his arms and I settle in the warmth of his comforting, protective embrace.

I could collapse and fall asleep right now. I could drift away in this perfect, blissful, easy contentment. I would always be safe with him, but I don't want that.

I trace my fingers over his chest. His chiseled torso looks so much bigger with his shirt off. He's a lot bigger than I realized.

I let my hand glide down his stomach. He stiffens when I touch him through his pants. This is the first time he's let himself show any response to me touching him.

I look up at him and he looks down at me at the same time. Our eyes lock the way they did in the limo.

Now I'm the one who holds his gaze while I unbuckle his belt, slide his zipper down, and pull him out of his shorts. He strains in my hand when I close my fingers around him.

He lets me see his breath hitching and his nostrils flaring when I stroke him in deep, masterful pumps. He feels thick, solid, and blasting hot like this. I could touch him like this all night long.

He doesn't let me, though. He adjusts his position so he doesn't stop me from touching him while he pushes his pants the rest of the way down and kicks them off. I keep the same rhythm until he lies back.

He lies there in my hand, rolls toward me, and kisses me while I stroke him raging hard. He doesn't try to stop me until he turns both of us on our sides.

Then he starts that slow, rhythmic pumping, grinding action with his hips that he used in the bar. He thrusts into my hand exactly as if we were doing it right now. I want him doing that inside me.

I spread my legs a little wider, drape one thigh over his side, and steer him between my legs. I rub his throbbing head through the swollen tissues he's just been preparing for himself. Our eyes never leave each other for an instant. He sees that I want this.

His fingers find me and delve inside. He plunges all the way in and makes me scream, but my wide, staring eyes have to keep searching the depths of his being until I discover all that he is.

He works his shaft through my hand in time to his own deep, fingering thrusts. He cycles me up to another climax, and at the peak of rapture when I can't stop tossing and struggling on his hand, he pushes past my grasp and eases in.

I grab him in a death grip, but he doesn't stop, He pulls me on top of him and guides my hips down so I straddle him. My weight drills him into me still screaming and roaring in his mouth as we come together the way we both want to.

He keeps kissing me through it all. His eyes never leave me alone even for a second. He works his hips in maddening circles to electrify me even as I lie convulsing and trembling on top of him.

His hands cover every inch of my back, ass, and thighs. He pulls me into his thrusts, compresses the back of my neck to hold me in place, and works his thick slab deep into my core to excite every nerve.

I want to crumble in front of him. I want to collapse on top of him and find safety in his arms—except that I already have it. He's inside and I'm riding down on him while he pumps into me from below.

I cascade again and again into oblivion. It never stops, not even when he rolls me onto my back and lies down on top of me.

He doesn't push up on his arms. He holds me in a tight embrace while we kiss, stretches all his weight on top of me, and screws into me the way he did in the bar.

I can't cope with this. I scream again and again, clamp my eyes shut to take the torturous explosions, and fight in every possible way to contain and release this energy at the same time.

It builds to a breaking point and detonates me in screaming madness before he winds it up to do it again. I can't take much more of this, but the energy keeps spiraling me out of control again and again until I just can't stop.

He pulls me back on top of him and I completely fall apart in his arms. I sink into his chest. I can't move even when he keeps pulsing inside me. He hasn't even come close to releasing his own tension. How much longer can he go?

Kevin pulls my head down on his shoulder, kisses my hair, and pets it out of the way to comfort me against his neck. I hide in that dark, excruciating place as all that explosive energy tries in every possible way to de-escalate and calm down.

It can't de-escalate as long as he stays hard and embedded in my deepest being. His body drives me insane. I already feel myself winding up and getting turned on again.

I push up to straddle him. He stares up at me from below while his hands keep exploring me, teasing me, stimulating me, and making me moan for more.

He grips my breasts, pinches and teases my nipples, rubs me between my legs to make me whimper, and pulls my thighs forward to drill himself deeper into me.

He watches me convulse on top of him for a minute. His movements trigger an answering response in me and I ride him faster to buck against his thrusts.

He sits up in one motion, scoops me up in his arms, and pivots onto his knees with me still strapped around him. He sits me on his brutal, straining shaft and pumps into me from below until I explode in another shrieking orgasm.

He doesn't stop. He keeps pounding me up and up and up until my mind dissolves in so much madness that I'll never come down from this.

Chapter 20: Kevin

I sit up and swing my legs off the bed to put my feet on the floor. I don't look behind me at Paige lying sprawled across the mattress. The sheets and blankets half-twist, half-wrap around her naked body.

I did it with her. She's the first woman I've been with in years. How am I supposed to feel about that?

She's in my bed. She's in my bedroom in my apartment. How am I supposed to feel about that?

She's as immaculate in bed as I dreamed she would be. She's sweet, responsive, and delicious. My body feels fragile from doing it with her all night long—in every possible position. I'm barely holding it together even now—and it isn't from lack of sleep.

I want to do it with her again. I want to do it with her a thousand times, but maybe I can't handle that. I can't handle it now after only one night.

She's every bit as sweet in bed as she is in person. The person that she is is far more intoxicatingly irresistible to me than her body—which is absolutely mind-blowing in itself. How am I supposed to feel about that?

How am I supposed to feel about the fact that I brought a woman home to my apartment and spent the night with her for the first time in years—maybe even decades?

I don't regret doing it. I don't regret that it was her or that we're in business together and will have to deal with each other professionally after this. I don't regret any of that. I don't regret any of it at all.

I just don't know how to feel about any of this. I don't know how to feel about myself. I need her. That's the bottom line. I've been living alone and handling my business with every other person on the planet all this time.

I haven't needed anyone. That's basically the real reason I never brought anyone home or hooked up with anyone or even dated anyone. I didn't need it. I saw no reason to do any of it when I had so many other more important things to do and focus on.

I need her now. I need her forever. How am I supposed to do that when she's barely divorced? She probably doesn't need me. I might just have been an appetizer for her to go out and find the man she really wants. He's a lucky son of a bitch whoever he is.

I can't even feel jealous of the guy. I'm happy for him and I'm happy for her. I care about her too much. I want her to be happy and I know she would make any man happy.

She's too kind, generous, and open not to. She wouldn't give her heart to any man without genuinely trying to make him happy.

I got a nice little taste of her body. That's all I got to touch an angel for one night. That's the best I can hope for.

I think she might be asleep, but she either woke up when I sat up or she was already awake. She crawls over to me, wraps her arms around me, and crawls her hot, fierce mouth all over my back and sides.

She starts working her way up my back to my neck. She eventually wraps her arms around my chest, and rubs her warm, bare breasts across my back.

I shut my eyes in the overpowering sensation of how incredible she feels. She's been doing things like this ever since we met in the bar. She doesn't hesitate to touch me, suck me, and blanket me in her luscious presence.

I can't get enough of her, but I don't let myself turn around even though I ache to. She's already making me hard again by touching me and kissing me like this.

I shudder when I think about doing it with her again. Her energy blasts me out of my mind. I struggle to survive the intensity even as I need it just to keep living.

How am I supposed to feel about any of this? How am I supposed to go back to living my life when I need her this badly?

She bites my neck and strokes her hands all over my chest from behind. Her breath sears my skin and she gives a small little exclamation of appreciation when she sinks her mouth into my shoulder.

"What does it mean?" she murmurs in my ear from behind.

"What do you want it to mean?" I ask over my shoulder.

"What *can* it mean?" she asks.

I shrug. I try not to shrug her off, but she takes it to mean that anyway. She stretches out on her back on the bed and runs her hand up and down my back. "Are you mad at me?" she asks.

"Of course not." I can't even look at her. Looking at her hurts.

She waits a long time before she speaks again. "I'm okay with it if it was just last night. It doesn't have to be anything else if you don't want it to be."

I try not to squirm when I shrug again. "I know you probably want to take some time to rebuild your life. That's what you should do. You don't want to get all mixed up with anything right away after you just finalized your divorce."

"Okay," she murmurs. "I'm okay with that."

"Don't you have to go to work today?" I ask.

She rolls in my direction onto her side. She doesn't stop stroking my back. "I don't want to leave until you're ready." She snickers to herself. "You'll have to throw me out if you want to get rid of me."

"I don't want to get rid of you. You can stay as long as you want."

"Why are you sitting up there like that, then?" she asks. "Are you finished with me?"

"Never. I would never be finished with you."

I expect her to pull me back into bed or something like that. She goes silent for a minute and then props herself up on her elbow.

She lays her hand on my shoulder and then on my cheek. "Turn around and look at me, Kevin."

I turn and look at her. The sight of her stabs a knife into my heart.

"What does it mean?" she asks more forcefully than before. "What do *you* want it to mean?"

"I just told you. You want to take time to yourself and I understand that...."

"I don't *want* to take time to myself, Kevin—not from you. *You* said that. I didn't. If you want something from me....."

My eyes fall out of their sockets. "What do you mean—you don't want to take time to yourself *from me?!* What does this have to do with me?"

"Because you're you, Kevin," she insists. "I would feel a whole lot differently about having something with you than I would about going out and looking for someone else."

I frown at her. "I don't understand."

"I would definitely take some time to myself if I had to go out and look for someone else. I would want to make certain I didn't make the same mistake I made with Trent. I definitely do NOT want to take time to myself if we're talking about you. You're you, Kevin. I feel differently about you."

I furrow my brow. She is not saying what I think she's saying. "How do you feel about me?"

Now she's the one who stares at me with her eyes bugging out. She stares for a long time and then snorts at me. "Jesus Christ, Kevin!" she growls. "What do you think I'm saying? You're the best man I can think of. I would never go out and look for someone else if I thought I had a prayer with you. You're everything I've ever looked for in a man and everything I've ever wanted to be in a human being. You're like some kind of angel sent to Earth to save the human race or something."

"I am not!" I counter.

"Will you just listen to me? Just tell me now if you even want something with me—something more than a casual good time for one night—because if you do, then that's what I want, too. I wouldn't even begin to look as long as there was any chance. Do you get that now? You're the one I really want. Anyone else would be my second choice. Is that clear enough for you?"

I can't look at her. She isn't saying this to me.

I break away from her as gently as I can and go back to sitting on the edge of the bed and staring into space. How am I supposed to feel about this?

She only waits a second before she turns the other way and sits up on the other side of the bed. "There. Now you know how I feel. If you want to keep it casual or leave it at one night, that's fine with me. I promise I won't let this interfere with our business. You don't have to worry about me or this or any of it. I think you're the greatest,

Kevin. I've been telling you that since the beginning. I think you're the greatest man I could ever possibly get with. So you don't have to wonder how I feel or what I want. I'll just let myself out....."

I spin around fast. "No! Don't leave. Just.....just sit down, Paige....please."

She stands on the other side of the bed looking at me across the disheveled mattress and bedding. We did it on this bed and in this bed. We did it countless times last night.

I can't stand the thought of her walking out—not after what she just said. She would actually go downstairs, put on her clothes, and leave me alone if I wanted her to.

She would give me whatever I wanted—whatever I needed to make me feel better and to make me happy. She would do it for the man in her life and that's what she wants me to be. She would do it for me even if it meant walking away from me.

She stands there stark naked and totally without shame. She doesn't register that she's showing me her naked body again—the body she gave to me for my pleasure.

I hold out my hand to her. "Please....just sit down....please."

She sits down on the bed with one knee folded so she can face me. She still doesn't even realize that I'm seeing her breasts, hips, ass, and her swollen flesh exposed for my eyes only.

She doesn't restart the conversation. That's up to me now. She said her piece. How am I supposed to feel about what she said?

"I.....I want that, too......" I struggle to control my voice and fail. "I want that."

"You want what?" she demands. "What is it that you do want?"

"You," I choke. "I want you....and not for one night and not for casual. I want......all of that."

How did I become so tongue-tied all of a sudden? I can't even tell her how I feel.

I can't look at her, either. I turn and face the other way. I shouldn't turn my back on her—not when I'm about to say these things.

I don't even know what I'm going to say until the words come out of their own accord. "You.....you're the greatest thing I've ever met—the greatest woman.....I never thought I would meet someone like you.....I've been telling myself all along that you were in another league....first you were married and then you were going through a divorce and now.....now I just keep telling myself you'll find someone else—someone who fits you better than I do—the person you actually want to get with. I know it doesn't make any sense. I just have a hard time breaking out of that."

"What is it you're saying you want from me?" she asks.

"I just told you. I want everything."

She doesn't answer right away. I can't bring myself to turn around no matter what I do. I said those words. Does she even realize how much I need her? I shouldn't have said that. I shouldn't put that much pressure on her so soon after her divorce.

She doesn't answer for so long that I get a sinking feeling in my gut. She turns the other way, sits on the opposite side of the bed, and faces outward with her back to me.

"I understand why you probably don't want that," I go on. "I'm okay with it. Really."

"What if I said I did want it?" Her voice shakes. "What if I said I want everything, too? What would we do then?"

I frown to myself. She isn't seriously saying that. Is she?

"Is that what you want?" I ask.

"I......" She hesitates and then lowers her voice to a broken half-whisper. "I guess it is. Yeah. It is." She turns around and stares at my back. "What does it mean?"

The tremor in her voice twists my heart. I have to look up at her. "I don't know. I don't know what it means."

Her eyes dart around the room. "Does that mean....does that mean I should leave? Does that mean.....?" She stares at me in pure terror. "What does it mean?"

"I don't know. I guess we just....you know.....keep going."

"But how? *How* do we keep going? Do we.....?" She glances down at my body like she just now noticed that we're both naked and that we just spent all night in this bed together. "What do we do?"

I extend my hand across the bed to take hers. "I don't know. I don't know what we do or what it means or what's going to happen. Just.....stay."

She opens her mouth, but no sound comes out. She looks as stunned and helpless as I feel, but at least I'm holding her hand now. We're doing.....something. Just don't ask me what that will be.

I squeeze her hand. "Why don't you go out to dinner with me next Friday? We can call it our first date."

She nods, but her eyes keep drifting off in other directions. She doesn't see anything in front of her.

I squeeze her hand one last time to get her attention. "Why don't you go in there and take a shower? I'll go downstairs and bring your clothes up here so you can get dressed. It's already too late for us to go into work today, so why don't we spend the day together here and just hang out? Then I'll take you home tonight and we'll go on as before until I can take you on a real date on Friday. Will that work?"

She nods at nothing. That's the best we can hope for at the moment since neither of us has a flippin' clue what we're doing here.

We're both grown adults and neither of us knows how to start having a relationship with each other. I don't even know what that would look like when she's as busy, driven, and successful as I am.

We wouldn't be the first or the last. Niko does it. Lane and Samantha do it. Dante and Emberlynn do it. Hell, they all do it. Why do I think it would be any different for me and Paige?

I don't like to think about something between us actually going that far—as in marriage. Could I really marry her and build a life with her? Why not? Everyone else is already doing it.

The number of club members' wives who are successful executives and operators vastly outnumbers the wives who aren't. Mckenna Pearson Metcalf isn't one and her relationship with Jackson works.

All the rest of them run their own companies. Some of these women are running multiple companies and even whole empires. Why should Paige be any different?

Why do I think it wouldn't work between us just because it's me and I've been alone all this time?

Chapter 21: Kevin

I have to show Paige where the bathroom is. It's in another room adjacent to this one with a big, deep, jacuzzi set into the tile floor, a wet-floor shower, sauna, and etched glass windows letting in natural light from outside.

I leave her there, put on a pair of sweatpants, go downstairs to get her dress, and put my clothes away. She's already in the shower. I pretend not to see her naked body through the water droplets on the glass door.

I leave her clothes out for her on the bathroom sink vanity and go downstairs to make her lunch. It's already ten o'clock.

She comes down fully dressed the way she was last night. I guess I can't expect her to just move in with me after one night—but I want her to. I don't want her to leave—ever.

I almost get the sense that I bought this apartment and kept it like this so she could come here. The apartment doesn't really make sense without her in it. I would never need this much space just for me.

It would be too big for the two of us, but maybe we might actually have a family at some point. Jesus, did I just think that? I really need to stay realistic. Paige and I aren't even dating yet.

I take a shower while she eats lunch. I change into something casual that she won't see as too slouchy.

She shoots me a look when I come downstairs and find her at the kitchen counter. "Now I feel really overdressed."

I cast one glance at her figure and find myself looking away. I have to bite back a grin. "There is no such thing when it comes to you."

"Do you get women interested in you?" she asks.

My head shoots up. "Why do you ask that?"

"I'm curious. I would assume all the men in the club get women throwing themselves at them all the time. Does that happen to you?"

"Throwing themselves at me? No, it doesn't happen. You are the first and only woman who has ever made a move on me—ever."

She raises her eyebrows. "Interesting. I wouldn't have expected that."

"Why not? Maybe the media hype isn't an accurate portrayal of what billionaire life looks like. I don't see women throwing themselves at the other guys, either."

"None of them?" she asks.

I shuffle my feet. "Well, not the married ones. Single women throw themselves at the single guys all the time. Some of the single guys encourage it, which leads to more of them doing it. Maybe that's the point. I don't encourage it, so they don't do it."

"I find it surprising that no one even expresses interest in you. You're young, handsome, single, and obviously filthy rich. I would have expected them to at least try it and for you to have to make it clear that you weren't interested."

I look away. "Can we talk about something else?"

She smiles at me. "Sure. What would you like to talk about?"

"Did you have a logical endpoint in mind when you started SigmaTech? Did you think you would sell it or just keep it going until the wheels fell off?"

She laughs. "I didn't think at the time that I would even make it into a company. I wasn't trying to start a company. I wasn't even trying to make money. I was just exploring, doing research, and trying to solve a few medical mysteries. It took me a long time to get it through my head that it was turning into a company that needed employees and budgets and customer support teams and all of that. I didn't want it to become that, but I eventually made the leap because that's what the patients needed the company to be. A lot of patients needed this equipment and making SigmaTech into a company was the only way to get the patients the treatment they needed. I wouldn't have done it otherwise." She frowns at me. "Why do you ask that?"

"I'm curious about you. I want to find out how your brain works. That's just me. I'm a people person."

She grins at me. "I got that."

I walk around the counter toward the stairs. "What would you like to do today?"

"I won't ask you what there is to do in this place. The only thing I really want to do is talk to you, so I really don't care what we do as long as we spend time together."

I laugh. "So you want to interview me? Is that it?"

"Of course. You've been interviewing me. Isn't that what we're here for—to get to know each other and see if this can go anywhere?"

"Come upstairs with me. We can interview each other there."

She follows me up to the fireplace sitting area. She seems the most comfortable there, but when we get up there, I see her eyeing the area closer to the windows. Maybe the fireplace area reminds her of us making out there last night.

The sitting area by the windows is sunnier anyway, so we go over there and sit down across from each other on the couches. "So...." I begin.

Her eyes twinkle at me. "So."

"Tell me what you're looking for in terms of your pay package with this company."

She bursts out laughing. "I'll settle for sexual favors."

I bite back a grin and my cheeks flush. "We might be able to work something out."

"Tell me about your past employment experience in this area," she counters.

My smile evaporates. "Experience—in relationships?"

"Yes. What is your experience? You know all about mine, unfortunately."

"I don't know about your experience before you got together with Trent."

She grins back at me. "I asked you first. You said you dated before you started People, Inc."

"Yes, I did."

"How did that go?"

I shrug. "I was young and stupid as most men are at that age."

"Was this during your community college and pizza parlor days?"

"Yes. I enjoyed myself back then."

"When would you say you stopped all of that?"

I look away and wind up staring out the window. I really don't want to talk to her about any of this, but I kind of backed myself into a corner here, didn't I?

"I'm sorry, Kevin," she exclaims. "You don't have to talk about it. I shouldn't have asked you something so personal."

"No!" I turn around. "I want to. I had three girlfriends during that time. Each one lasted about a year, but none of them was serious. We just went out and enjoyed ourselves. We never talked about getting any more serious than that. Then People, Inc. took off and I just didn't get around to looking very hard after my last relationship broke up. I guess I just kept not looking."

She frowns at me. "So you haven't seen anyone in all that time?"

"Nope."

"You haven't even hooked up with anyone?"

I snort at her. "I don't do that. I wouldn't waste my time with something like that." I frown at her. "Do you?"

"Well, I've been married for the last seven years. You're the first person I've been with since Trent—if that's what you mean."

"And before that? Did you date before Trent?"

Now she's the one who looks away like she doesn't want to talk about it. "I had a boyfriend before Trent."

"Just one boyfriend? Is that all?"

She nods toward the window. She won't look at me.

"What's wrong?" I ask. "Don't tell me he ended up dead, too."

"No, he's still alive and well and working at Chicago General Hospital. He was in medical school while we were going out. We actually lived together. He was one of the very few people who thought my research and experimental machines was a good idea. He encouraged me a lot—and then he graduated and moved to Chicago. He got offered his dream job, so he left to take and we agreed that it would be better if we went our separate ways and didn't drag each other down. He had already been struggling to spend enough time with me while he was in medical school. He didn't think he could do the relationship justice while he was an intern and then a resident, so we decided to call it quits. Then I ended up with Trent."

"*How* did you end up with Trent? How did you go from that to Trent?"

She shrugs. She still won't turn around. I regret asking her this now. "He didn't outright discourage my work back then. He thought it was a quirky hobby—which is all it was back then. I didn't really take it seriously because it hadn't developed into anything more than that. I went to school for accounting and that's what I did for a day job. We had a normal life where I worked on my research and messing around with my machines after work and on the weekends like other people might build model airplanes or something like that. I worked on them at the living room coffee table while we watched movies or TV or just shot the breeze about our days at work. It wasn't anything either of us took seriously and I never thought it would ever become anything serious. That developed later."

"So do you see red flags now that you should have spotted at the time? What would you do differently if you could go back and do it over again?"

She finally turns to face me and shoots me a grin. "Now you really sound like you're interviewing me for a place in your life."

"Not at all. You already have that."

She blushes. "I don't think I should have, would have, or could have done anything differently. I don't think there were any red flags I should have spotted. I think I changed. I know I changed. I outgrew the relationship and that made him extremely defensive because he saw that I was becoming less and less compatible with him. He saw that I was moving into a completely different category of life. I was becoming someone completely different from the person I was when I got together with him. I wasn't satisfied with the things I was satisfied with when I got together with him. So maybe I was the one throwing up red flags." She cocks her head at me. "Does that answer your question?"

"Yes, it does." I stand up. "Let's go out for a walk."

"I thought you wanted to spend the day in here."

"I changed my mind. Come on. We can stop by your place and you can change into something more appropriate."

I walk over to her and take her hand to lead her out of the apartment. I want to get out into the world with her.

I want to walk through Central Park and feel her next to me. I don't know why, but staying inside this apartment doesn't satisfy what I really want to do with her—which is everything.

I don't know where this is going and I don't even really need to know that anymore. I just want more of her—a lot more. I want to explore all of this and I want to explore the whole world with her.

She turns to follow me toward the elevator, but I have to stop her there to kiss her. She's just too damn appealing to me. I want to feel her against me one more time.

She wraps her arms around me and melts into my lips. Her fingers thread into my hair and her smell hits me like a freight train right in the head. She intoxicates me.

All thought of going out into the world vanishes out of my mind the minute I kiss her. I wind my arms around her waist and lift her against me. She feels it, too, and her breath catches in her throat.

I squeeze her tighter and her body shivers in my arms. That feeling reminds me of everything we did last night and so much more to come. I can't stop myself from touching her.

I can't touch her while I'm holding onto her. I shift her weight and my hold on her so I can grab a handful of her ass—and then I know I have to have her. I turn her toward the wall, take a step, and pin her there.

She whimpers into my mouth. I know that sound. She wants it. She wants me to take her like this—right up against the wall. She gets this ravenous, insane kind of energy when she wants me to unleash and go primal on her.

I yank her dress up and raise her legs around my waist. She escalates to match me and I drill right up against her. We're both panting so fast I can't kiss her anymore.

I cram my forehead against her glaring down into her eyes. She grabs me and rips my shirt open, but she can't get to me any more than that.

That moment when she exposes my chest breaks the dam on all our passion. She's mine. I'm going to make her mine. I have to. I have to have her—all of her.

I tear my fly open and slam into her to make her scream. I dreamed of this when I pressed up against her in the bar. I imagined doing it to her just like this and watching her crawl up the wall with every pounding thrust.

We both rasp through bared teeth. Her sex-drunk eyes float up to meet mine and don't look away. I grab her breasts, her ass—any part of her I can get my hands on.

I dive into her neck and consume every fragrant lungful of her scent. Her soft, hot wetness clamps down on me and won't let me go.

I let loose on her in all my power. She screams louder and takes it harder.

She spasms underneath me, but that only spurs me to hit her harder. Every scream spirals me out of my mind. I can't get enough. To hell with the outside world. She's all mine and I'll never let her go.

Chapter 22: Paige

Kevin lies on his side next to me resting his head and torso against his pile of pillows. He strokes his tender fingertips down my cheek to my neck, down my arm and sides to my thighs, and back up. He keeps gliding back and forth endlessly.

"We'll need to get up soon," he murmurs. "I need to take you home this morning. You have to work and so do I. We can't spend all our time in this bedroom banging each other."

I blush and turn my face downward into the pillow. "Why can't we?"

"We agreed you would go home and we would try to have a normal week before our date on Friday. We've already wasted the entire day and another night."

"Was it really wasted?"

"No, of course not," he murmurs. "I didn't mean that."

"I can't help it if I find you irresistible,"

"I find you irresistible, too, sweetheart," he breathes. "Don't you know that by now?"

I gaze up into his eyes. They glow out of the semi-darkness. It's almost dawn on the second morning. We've been here for two nights and a whole day just drinking each other in as much as we can.

"Just promise me it won't be casual," I tell him. "Promise me you want it to be real the same way I do."

"It could never be casual between us," he murmurs. "That doesn't exist between us."

I bow my head and close my eyes. I want too much with him. Just looking at him makes my heart ache for more even when I have him right here in front of me.

I don't want to just spend the night with him or even days and nights in bed. I want everything with him just as he wants it with me. We both want that, so why do we have to go back to our separate lives?

I know we have to do this the right way. I know we have to date and all of that. I just want all of him now.

I know he feels the same way. He rakes his fingers through my hair, clasps me behind the head, and kisses me on the forehead. He's always so tender and caring even when he gets rough.

His body casts a spell on me. I really can't resist him. I have no choice but to respond every time he wants me. His touch and his kiss bring me back every time no matter how often or how many times we do it.

He pulls me against him and I fall into his embrace like I was born to be here. I don't want to be anywhere else—but I guess I have to be.

The sky keeps getting lighter outside the windows. We can see each other more clearly now—or we could if we weren't holding onto each other so tightly.

I don't hold onto him out of any sexual desire even though that's all still there. I just want to hold him. I want to feel him near me. I feel safe with him—much safer than I've ever felt with any other man or even by myself. I don't want to lose that.

Some part of me dreads that I will lose him if I look away just for an instant. I can't let that happen—but he's right that we can't stay in bed all the time.

Having a life with him or a relationship with him or even exploring what a relationship with him would mean—all of that means we deal with real life together.

We eventually pull apart and lie on our sides facing each other. It would be so easy to fall into each other's bodies the way we have been. We would pant and climax and hold onto each other and fill each other with so much ecstasy.

None of that even comes close to the togetherness of just lying here and looking into each other's eyes. His eyes overflow with so much unspoken communication. I know he feels the same way looking back at me.

The sun peeks over the buildings outside. I don't want to turn around to see, but it casts its first golden rays through the windows onto the opposite wall. The light in the room changes. It's daytime now.

He leans in and kisses me. It's a light, sensual, heartfelt kiss because we both know this little blissful interlude is ending. I don't want to look away from those eyes. I don't want to get out of this bed, but I have to.

We both smile at each other and sit up at the same time. I go take a shower while he goes downstairs to make breakfast.

He must have another shower somewhere because he's standing at the kitchen counter fully dressed in a suit with his hair combed and all his accessories in place by the time I come downstairs.

We sit and chat at the counter while we eat. "Don't make any excuses to come over to People, Inc. to supervise the trainer training program this week," he tells me. "I'll know you're getting desperate if you show up there."

I laugh at him. "It's too bad you don't have any excuses to come over to the SigmaTech building. Then we could at least gaze at each other across a crowded room."

"Are you sure I don't have any excuses? Do you need any staff?"

I blush and grin at him. "You would be the first person I called if I did."

"Are you sure you wouldn't call me for something else?"

We share a knowing look and we both laugh. I would love to call him for that. It's going to be a long week.

He escorts me to the elevator and we ride down to the garage. The driver is already seated behind the limo's tinted windows with the engine running.

"Don't you ever see his face?" I ask once we get into the car and head off down the street.

"Sure. That's Rashid."

"Does he work for you?"

"No, he works for the limo service that drives me around, but I always request him. We understand each other."

"He doesn't get offended that you don't talk to him?"

"I do talk to him—just not when you're around. I don't want him watching what I'm doing with you."

I glance up at him and he leans in to give me a small kiss. Rashid the limo driver drops me off outside my apartment building and I rush upstairs to change for work. I really need to get a regular limo driver who knows when and where to pick me up and drop me off.

I somehow struggle through the rest of the day and then the next one. Thinking about Kevin drives me insane, especially when we have to communicate about our business dealings.

We're both going into negotiations with Diego and the generals, so Kevin and I have to talk a lot on the side about how to present our offering in the best way.

Neither of us mentions our time together in his apartment or the fact that we're supposed to be going on a date on Friday night. My nerves are starting to get the better of me.

I've also spent entirely too much time playing with myself in the privacy of my bedroom this week. I want to tell him so—to tease him and give him something to think about, but I decide against it each time. I want to be professional in professional contexts.

Would it ever get like that between us? Would we ever get so serious about each other that we would send each other sexual texts and messages during the week? That would be so freakin' hot. I would love that.

Fantasizing about him makes the rest of the week a torturous wait. I'm a nervous wreck by the time Friday rolls around. Where is he planning to take me? Will we be going home to his place afterward?

I resist the urge to ask him if I should bring my toothbrush and a change of clothes for tomorrow. I don't want to assume anything.

I take a long time to decide what to wear. He seems to appreciate anything that shows off my figure, so I go with a drape neckline cream dress with angled creases running the length down to my shins.

I admire myself in the mirror before it's time for him to pick me up. I look damn good. I like the way I look. I would date me if I was a guy. I giggle at the thought and get back to the more important business of putting on my jewelry and getting ready to go.

Chapter 23: Paige

Kevin shows on at exactly the right time. He always looks outstanding in impeccable suits with every detail in the right place. He wears suits easily. He's comfortable in them and they make him look fantastic.

Sure enough, his eyes widen and glide down my body when I open the door. "Is that your way of luring me inside?" he asks.

"Is it working?"

He laughs and turns away blushing. "I'll avert my eyes—like Perseus did with Medusa."

I laugh along with the joke and take his arm on our way to the elevator. "So where are we going?"

"I thought we would do the old traditional go-out-to-dinner thing—if that's all right with you."

"That would be great. What are we going to talk about tonight?"

"Do you have any hobbies outside of work?"

"Doing my research and developing these machines was always my hobby before it became my job. It still is both. I still do research on the side to find new ways to treat diseases and new equipment we could develop. I guess that part of it has always been my main focus. The business side of it was never my main interest. I understood the accounting part, but I had to learn how to run the business itself. What about you?"

"The club is my hobby."

I spin around. "Are you one of the founders?"

"No, no. Not by a long shot—but the club and its many functions seem to take the place of a hobby in my life—apart from People, Inc, of course. The company has always been a combination of work and a hobby for me, too." He cocks his head to study me. "You seem to run the business just fine."

"I'm the one with the vision about why this equipment is so needed. I'm the driver that pushes the company to help more and more people. That's what keeps the company growing and expanding and that comes from me. I'm talking about the marketing, hiring—all of that. I would just as soon skip it and stay in my lab doing my own thing."

We pause our conversation long enough to get into the limo. He shoots me a smirk on the side. "I envision you as some kind of mad scientist with huge, magnifying glasses attached to your eyes and your hair sticking out in a halo around your head while you tinker in your lab."

I laugh. "Tell me if I ever get like that. Tell me to go to the mall and go shopping for a while to get my head back to reality."

He gazes up at me. "So are you going to have a home lab set up at the apartment?"

I jolt in my seat. "Um....what?"

He looks away. "Forget I said that. What I meant was..... do you have a home lab set up at your apartment?"

"I won't forget you said it, and no, I don't have a lab set up at my apartment. I do research on the computer at my apartment and do the tinkering and lab work at the office when I can pry myself away from all my meetings and everything. Sometimes I go down there on my lunch break if I don't have anything else scheduled."

"I would love to see some of your stuff."

"But you're a people person. You don't do all that."

"I want to see you in your native habitat and study your behaviors and native rituals."

I laugh again just as the limo pulls up in front of another large restaurant. Kevin escorts me inside. The downstairs main room is packed with patrons all talking at once. The place is stuffy and noisy.

He has to yell into the maître d's ear to make him hear what Kevin wants. The guy nods and waves us to a set of stairs on one side. Kevin keeps his arm behind me and his hand resting on my back on the way upstairs.

That touch tells me loud and clear that we're together. There is nothing casual about this. He's announcing the fact to the world we're here as a couple.

It's much quieter upstairs and the atmosphere much more ambient. We can barely hear the noise down there.

The maître d' seats us at an intimate, candlelit table by the windows overlooking Park Avenue. The glamor of all the stores casts an almost artistic frame around people and cars passing below us.

Kevin takes my hand and gazes at me across the table. "This is nice. I like being out with you."

"I like being out with you, too." I squeeze his hand. "I've always liked your company. We don't always have to spend our time in bed."

"It's nice to know we still have it even after what happened."

I laugh at him. "You make it sound like a natural disaster or federal emergency or something."

He grins and his cheeks color. "Maybe it was kind of like that."

"Do you think you'll stay in New York forever?" I ask. "Do you like it here enough to stay?"

He shrugs. "It seems to work. Staffing will always be in demand and I have a captive audience with the other billionaires. I'm always the first person they call when they need people. I'm always the first person everyone calls when they need people."

"I'm not surprised. You've made yourself invaluable to everyone."

"I get contracts from all over the country—and now this deal with Niko is going international. Who knows where it could lead? So I don't only work in New York. This is just the head office." He cocks his head. "Hmm. That gives me ideas about expanding into other areas."

"But getting back to my questions....are you happy here—happy enough to stay? Do you think you'll always live here?"

"I don't see why not. The club is here. All my friends are here. My work is here and I've already established a network here. I know enough people here and I have a base of support. It would take me a long time to reestablish that somewhere else. It's like I told you. I never thought about having anything else. What I have has always been enough." His eyes lock on me. "What about you? Do you think you'll stay in New York? Do you think you'll ever go home?"

"I doubt it. Things weren't ideal there and they're so much better here. Besides, Trent is back there—and SigmaTech is here. So it isn't really a contest, is it?"

The waiter comes and takes our order. He also delivers us a bottle of wine and some bread.

"Where do you see SigmaTech going in the next ten years?" Kevin asks.

I laugh. "Now there's an interview question if I've ever heard one. I would like to see us in every hospital and maybe every doctor's office in the country and maybe even the world. I would like to see all the militaries and foreign aid organizations using our equipment. I would like to see SigmaTech start to shape and mold the future of modern medicine so we don't get stuck in the past. I don't think the medical field is nearly innovative enough."

He raises his eyebrows. "Many people would disagree."

"Many people would be wrong. Many people wouldn't realize how entrenched the medical field is in the status quo and doing things the old way. The medical field is slower to adopt innovation than anyone else even though adopting it would mean saving patients' lives. The medical field is the most resistant to change or even to admitting that change is possible. Trust me. No one is more familiar with this process than I am." I grimace. "Sorry. I'll try not to turn our dates into promotional speeches."

"I love how passionate you are about all of this. It's one of your most attractive qualities."

I look away. "It does have a tendency to get me into trouble."

"That's because you aren't talking to the right people. I'm sure there arc plenty of people like your first boyfriend who think what you're doing is awesome and that you're an exceptional person for doing it."

"Where do you see People, Inc. going in the next ten years?" I ask.

He frowns to himself and swirls his wine in his glass. "It's interesting. If you had asked me that just an hour ago or even half an hour ago, I would have said I wanted People, Inc. to just keep expanding our client and recruitment pool, to keep investing in people, and to keep growing our market segment."

"What's wrong with that?"

"Nothing is wrong with it except that sitting here talking to you is making me think bigger than that. I can see how it could be even bigger and even better than it already is. We could actually be changing lives."

"How would you do that? You're already changing lives. You're changing a lot of lives."

"But think about it." He points at me. "Think about that young man I was supposed to meet last weekend and didn't. I could be helping people like that—a lot more people like that—or the company could be. We could expand our offering to provide professional development for our people to level up and improve their lives. We could offer our client companies the option that we could hire in unqualified people who have a good work ethic and a history of successful, reliable employment. They would just need additional training to qualify for whatever position the company is recruiting for. Then we could provide the training and get the person qualified for an even higher ranked or higher paying position. See? Or we could offer programs to get young kids out of the ghetto or out of juvenile hall or prison or wherever and into training programs that would qualify them for these sought-after jobs. That would give the kids a vehicle to get them off the street and keep them out of prison. Or we could offer some other kind of program to people like this young man who are trapped in dead-end jobs who want a way out. They could segue from their current job and into a paid training program that would either turn into a permanent job or lead to one."

I stare at him across the table. "Did you just come up with that right now—while we're sitting here?"

"Yes, of course. Do you think I thought of it before? I would already be doing it if I had thought of it before. You inspired me by talking about helping more people and changing more lives. That's what you do, but we could be doing the same thing—I mean we could be doing more of it on a mass scale. That's what I would like to do. We're thinking small right now. We're changing lives one person at a time, but we could be doing that at scale with our whole company all over the country and maybe even the world."

I'm still blinking at him in disbelief when our waiter comes with our food. I don't know what else to say to Kevin.

He asks me about our joint deal between SigmaTech and People, Inc. on one side and Diego and the generals on the other, so we talk about that for the rest of the meal.

Kevin gathers me in his arms in the back of the limo on our way home. "You give me new energy," he murmurs between kisses. "You inspire me to do even more. This is going to be wonderful. I just know it."

"Are you talking about the deal, your new training program idea, or what's going on between us?"

He smiles at me. "All of it. I'm happy about all of it—and I'm really happy about you. You're wonderful, too."

We both sink into kissing each other, but that kiss inevitably leads to more. His hands start to range all over my body—and then my hands start to range all over his body.

I slide my hand between his legs to touch him. He pulls off my mouth and stares deep into my eyes while I stroke him, but he doesn't take it any further than that nor does he try to stop me.

His hot, commanding hand clamps on my thigh just high enough to give me a volcanic rush of heat between my legs.

"I would love to take you home and take you in my bed all night long," he breathes.

"I want that, too."

He shakes his head. "Not tonight. We're doing this by the book. We need to get to know each other better first. I want our dates to be real dates that lead to more. I don't want to turn them into foreplay sessions."

I can't help but grin at them. "But I like foreplay sessions."

"We'll have plenty of time for that."

Like magic, the limo pulls up in front of my building just then. Kevin and I stay in the seat kissing in long, dreamy, succulent passion for another fifteen minutes before he catches my eye.

"We have another negotiation this week," he tells me. "I'll see you then."

"What will happen between us at the negotiation?"

"Nothing will happen between us at the negotiation because we'll be there to negotiate, not for anything to happen between us."

I pretend to give him a military salute. "Yes, Sir."

"Behave yourself. I'll be watching."

I kiss him one more time. "I can't wait to see you again."

He responds by squeezing my ass once before I get out of the limo and rush inside. I'm going to see him again in a few days.

Chapter 24: Kevin

I feel myself starting to get heart palpitations going into the negotiation with Diego and the generals. I don't care about the negotiation. I'm about to see Paige again.

I'm having a harder and harder time keeping our communication professional. I can only imagine how hard it's going to be to sit in the same room with her without tearing her clothes off.

I won't even be able to look at her body—not without getting distracted. I have to pay attention to the negotiation. I have to pay attention to the deal itself and the people on the other side of the table—not the person sitting next to me.

This will be the first time I've gone into a negotiation like this with these feelings hanging over my head. I've never had a problem keeping my professional life professional.

Paige is making my life a lot more complicated than it needs to be, but she's so damn appealing that I can't resist. I don't know where this is going, but something has to give.

I just need her in my bed and in my apartment all the time—around the clock. That's the bottom line. I can't keep living with the uncertainty of what's going on between us or when I'll see her or how far it will go.

I need to know that I'll see her at home every night and that I'll have her in my bed whenever I want her. Then I can stop thinking about all of this and just continue to live my life.

Am I really thinking of her in those terms? I try to stay rational, especially in my dealings with her. We've gone on one date and I did actually manage not to nail her in the back of the limo. I wanted to, though. Damn, did I want to!

I've always disapproved of the guys who do stuff like that—unless they're married to the woman, of course. Then they can do what they want.

I never wanted to see myself as that guy. Now I see myself turning into that guy—or I could turn into that guy if I didn't keep myself on a tight leash.

I want to be one of the married guys who can get away with that because he knows she's his woman. That's what I really want. I want to be able to take her any way, anyhow, anywhere because she's mine and no one can tell me not to.

No one can criticize how or where or when the guys take their wives because they're already established couples. That's what I want. I want that certainty. I don't want to guess and date and wonder anymore if what I'm doing is appropriate or sleazy or disrespectful.

I have to go into a separate room, shut my eyes, and take a bunch of deep, steadying breaths before I walk into the conference room where I'm going to see Paige again.

We're meeting in a neutral location downtown so none of the parties to this negotiation is on their home turf. We aren't meeting in any of our own company buildings or anywhere any of the parties might consider themselves as acting as a host to the other parties.

Just the thought of going into the same room with her makes my body tense up. I'm not nervous about the negotiation. I'm excited because I'm going to be near her again. I'm excited because I want her.

The rest of my team waits for me in the hallway outside. I rejoin them. Can they all feel how jumpy I am? This isn't a good look at all. I'm usually the steadying influence on everyone else. Nothing shakes me, but she does.

We walk into the conference room and find Paige and the SigmaTech people already there. These aren't the same people from the training program. She's brought four other members of the SigmaTech executive team with her.

We go around the room shaking hands. Her eyes speak volumes when we shake hands. Is she as wound up as I am?

The energy coming from her makes me dizzy. We stand there talking casually for a minute before Diego and his people show up. Holy shit, I want to kiss her right now. I want to put my hand on her back and let her and everyone else in the room know that she's mine.

I can't do that here. How the hell am I supposed to get through this negotiation?

The other people in the room save us from each other. We both have to talk to everyone else about what's happening and all our other dealings with each other's businesses.

The other SigmaTech execs want to thank me and congratulate me on the trainer training program. We use that to smooth things over until Diego arrives.

The greetings take a long time. I don't have to talk to Paige again, but I become painfully aware of her presence across the room. I find myself watching her movements, behaviors, and interactions with every other man present.

I'm watching her as though I'm already the man in her life. I keep an eye on her—not because I'm jealous. She's never given me any reason to be.

I'm watchful of the way other men in the room act toward her. Diego hugs her and kisses her on both cheeks in a very European way. They stand close to each other and chat, but it's purely friendly banter.

I see her blushing and grinning at things he says, but that's just the normal, friendly, bubbly response she has to talking to anyone, especially someone she knows well.

They've been talking non-stop since she moved to New York. They've been emailing, having video conferences, and she's been talking to him in person at the club and every other place she sees him in public.

The guy has the moves, though. I have to give him that. He's a charmer when it comes to the ladies and he definitely lays on the charm with her.

She responds to it, but both of them keep it strictly platonic. It's obvious from their body language that neither of them considers this anything more than friendly banter between business associates.

The generals keep it much more neutral. She listens to everything they say with a thoughtful, interested expression, nods, and offers her input in return.

She mirrors everyone else's behavior and body language to exactly reflect whatever level of engagement they need from her.

I'm proud of her. I'm proud of how adept she is at matching all these people and putting them perfectly at ease.

I catch myself being proud of her as if she's already mine. I should stop myself from doing that. The clash between reality and what I want throws me off.

I do the same thing with everyone around me. I talk to them, reflect their level of engagement and seriousness, and fall straight back into my old ways of doing everything.

No one sees anything unusual about my behavior—because there isn't anything unusual about my behavior. My turmoil and uncertainty is all on the inside.

The time eventually comes for everyone to sit down at the table. Paige and I have to sit right next to each other with the SigmaTech team on her other side and the People, Inc. team on my other side.

We catch each other's eye as we sit down. Her eyes shoot a lightning bolt of adrenaline straight to my guts. I see in that one fleeting glance that she really is having as hard a time with this as I am. It's both of us. We're reacting to each other.

That one moment makes it a thousand times harder to sit next to her and keep my cool. Diego opens the negotiations and Paige and I start laying out our offering. She talks about the equipment SigmaTech will provide.

I talk about the trained personnel I'll provide and the programs we've been jointly running so far to bring all the personnel up to speed in time to roll out the equipment both to the military and our other contracts.

Diego and the generals ask a bunch of pointed questions. Paige and I have to exchange glances multiple times to answer and combine all the relevant information.

Then we present side-by-side cost comparisons between what we would charge our counterparties to purchase the equipment and train the personnel separately.

The crux of our offering is that no one can get this training from anyone other than People, Inc. No one in the entire sector is trained to use this equipment.

My company is the only company where the militaries can send their people for training. The military would either have to take this offering or purchase the equipment and training separately.

The price comparison is a no-brainer. The personnel are going to come to People, Inc. for training either way.

The counterparties might as well take the package offer. There's no reason for them not to. Paige and I have packaged the deal so our counterparties have no choice but to take it.

The generals and their staff ask a few more questions about roll-out options, making the equipment more mobile, and if that will affect the trainees' operation of the equipment in any way.

Paige and I have to hold a brief, whispered conversation about certain aspects of the subject. She leans extra close to me and I have to bend down to put my ear near her mouth.

I actually feel myself starting to get hard when she does that. This is such an intimate pose and brings up all kinds of memories from our time together.

I want her to whisper in my ear like that right before I tip her onto her back, pull up her skirt, and make her arch and moan in ecstasy.

Fortunately, the table hides my reaction. We both straighten up, face front, and I calm down through the rest of the negotiation. I don't have anything to worry about by the time we finish talking and stand up to shake hands.

Then we all stand around the conference room talking casually afterward before it's time to leave. Diego and the generals leave first.

The SigmaTech and People, Inc. teams meet out in the hall and everyone asks everyone else what they're doing after this. Some of them invite each other to lunch. They ask me and Paige to go with them. Paige and I exchange glances.

I make an excuse about needing to go back to the office. She does the same thing. That gets us out of it. The people going to lunch leave the building together. She shoots me one more meaningful glance and goes off in one direction. I go off in another.

I stop on that side of the building and text Rashid to come and pick me up. The building entrance doesn't offer enough space for him to pull up the limo. The building has a separate limo entrance with more space and a covered arch to protect the car from the weather.

I pass down a hallway and stop in a small vestibule right inside the limo driveway. I'm standing there checking my phone when Paige comes into the vestibule. She freezes for a second and then smiles. "Great minds think alike, huh? Are you waiting for Rashid?"

"I didn't know you rode in limos now. Is that new?"

She blushes so beautifully. "I'm trying on this whole billionaire thing for size. I'm not sure how I feel about it."

"It suits you." My desire for her becomes overwhelming and I slip my arm around her waist from behind. Just standing this close to her makes me hard. "That was the hardest negotiation of my life."

She gasps and then her lips fall against mine. "You handled it so much better than I did!" she pants. "You were so cool."

"I need you," I whisper. "I need you right now."

I can't stop myself from grinding against her. I want to feel her softness around me this instant. I can't wait any longer.

She moans in that deep, agonized longing that shoots straight to my nuts. I push her against the wall and then pull her into a side dressing room adjacent to the vestibule.

She won't stop whimpering in desperate need while I push her against a different wall and turn her backward to press into her from behind. She arches her ass into my prick and shivers when I rake her skirt up.

I plaster my mouth against her ear and snarl out all my broken, ravenous hunger for her. Standing this close to her is becoming the worst torture I can imagine.

She arches her back exactly the way I like it. I pin her under my weight, yank up her skirt, and tear my pants open.

She squeals when I drive into her from behind. I can't stop growling in her ear. I want her to hear what she does to me. I don't want to hold back. I want to treat her as mine and take her as mine.

I want doing it with her to be as legitimate as any of the married guys. Am I really thinking of her in that way? I want to. I want that. I want to think of her in those terms.

I want to look across the room at her working her business contacts and know that she's mine.

I want to look across the room and know that I'm the only man who gets to see her like this—unchained, insane, and blasting apart with more passion than she can cope with.

I am that man, so why shouldn't I call her mine? I still hesitate to put it in those terms. I don't want to scare her with how badly I need to possess her—and I don't just mean her body.

I want her in my house. I want her in my life. I don't want to do this alone anymore. I could handle doing it alone, but that was before I met her. I can't go back to that now.

She shrieks when I slam into her. She throws her head back and then crams her skull against mine as the wave shatters her apart. Her body thrashes and tosses under me. My instincts kick in and I hold her down even harder so she doesn't get away from me.

She plants her hands against the wall, claws at me, and struggles against her own overpowering energy. Her response triggers an answering explosion in me and I roar in her ear as all my aching need pours out into her.

She crushes me under the weight of so much emotion. I can't handle this. I need her too badly—and she doesn't even know it. She doesn't know I need her.

I don't want to let her go after it's all over. I want to stay buried inside her forever and never leave. I stroke into her milking the last exquisite, whimpering sighs from her sweet lips.

I keep my body against hers for as long as I can. I need to feel her here next to me. I need to feel our bodies together. It acts like some kind of medicine for something wrong with me—something I didn't know was wrong with me.

The only thing wrong with me is that I'm too far away from her—too far away emotionally, too far away in space. I need my life all tangled up with hers. I need to share one life between the two of us. I'll never be happy or complete without that.

I still can't tell her. I don't even know why. What would I tell her—that I want to marry her after one date and one brief hookup? I could never tell her that.

I kiss the side of her cheek and wind up crawling all over her face and neck. She sobs again when I do that. She turns her head to kiss me back. I already feel both of us cycling up to do it again.

My phone buzzes in my jacket pocket. Rashid is waiting for me outside and her driver is waiting for her.

I pull away and we barely make eye contact while we both straighten our clothes. Now I'm going to be walking around with her honey all over me for the rest of the day. This is a first. I don't want to repeat it—but how can I avoid it if I don't take her home with me?

The only reasonable solution is to take her home and keep her there. Then we can do it as much as we want to and still shower and change our clothes in time for work each morning. That's what I really want, so why shouldn't we have it?

The uncertainty of not knowing if she wants it drives me out of my mind. I can't even ask her.

I should. I should just come right out and propose to her. What the hell? Then I would at least know if she feels the same way.

That would be too desperate—proposing to her this soon. I want to. I need to, but I'll just have to wait and let some time pass. Why rush it if we're going to be spending the rest of our lives together?

Chapter 25: Kevin

Paige and I step out of the vestibule into the limo driveway where both of our limos wait for us. We barely look at each other or say a word of goodbye. The tension and subtext between us is becoming unbearable.

I get into my limo and she gets into hers. What a crime that is. She should be getting into my limo and kissing me on our way back to work. We should be exchanging knowing smirks while we tell each other we'll see each other at home later.

Home. I want my apartment to be her home. I want my bed to be her bed and my closet to be her closet. This distance between us is all wrong.

I have no choice but to blunder through the rest of the day and the rest of the week. Things have gotten so tense and awkward between us that I haven't even asked her out for a second date. I really hope she doesn't think I've changed my mind about her because of that.

We held the negotiation with Diego and the generals on Tuesday. I can't wait until the weekend. I suffer through another thirty-six hours of torture before I break down and cave to the pressure.

I wait for a lull in my workday on Thursday and take my phone into an unused conference room to call her.

She answers with a chirpy, "Hi there!"

"I need to see you," I blurt out in a husky undertone. "I'm going crazy over here."

Her voice changes instantly. "What's wrong?"

"I don't know. I just...I need to see you. Are you doing anything for lunch?"

"No, I'm not doing anything. Do you want to meet somewhere?"

I think fast and choose a restaurant equidistant between People, Inc. and SigmaTech. "How about the Boys from Brazil? It's on Seventh Avenue."

"Yeah, I know where it is. How about half an hour?"

"Okay. See you there."

I hang up and feel my hands shaking. I don't know what's happening to me, but I need to get some clarity on this whole thing with her. I just need a definite answer one way or the other so I can function.

I leave work right then. I don't want to pretend I'm okay when I'm not. I decide to walk to the restaurant just to burn off some of this nervous energy. I don't wind up spending the whole half hour pacing outside like a caged animal waiting for her to show up.

I get there ten minutes before I'm supposed to meet her, so I get a table in the back. Now comes the hard part.

She shows up exactly on time. Of course. That's her. She smiles when I stand up to greet her, but I definitely sense the anxiety radiating off her. I sure hope she doesn't think I brought her here to break up with her.

We both sit down. She gives the waiter a smile when he delivers our water and menus. Then she turns to me. "So what's going on?"

"That's what I want to know. What's going on between us? I'm going crazy from not knowing. I need to know where we're going and what this whole thing is."

"I thought you were clear on that. You said we would explore it and see where it goes."

"I know I said that." I have to stop and steady myself before I go on. "The uncertainty is driving me nuts. What happened between us at the negotiation...." I can't even say it.

She lowers her eyes for a second. "That probably shouldn't have happened."

"I mean.....do we even have a relationship or not?" I blurt out. "What are we supposed to do about it if we do have a relationship—because, if we don't, I would just as soon know right now so I can just go back to concentrating on work. I can't keep getting pulled off track by thinking about this."

"Is that what it's doing—pulling you off track? I don't want that. I don't want anything between us to derail your career. That's the last thing I want. If that's the case, then maybe we should put the whole thing on ice until things cool down and we can proceed in a more rational way without all these loaded expectations."

"I don't mean the relationship is pulling me off track. I don't mean that at all. I want a relationship with you. I mean thinking about it and worrying about it and being uncertain about if it even is a relationship is pulling me off track. Like...if we have one, then there's no reason why we should keep tiptoeing around pretending we don't. We would be able to go into a business negotiation without getting all worked up over the fact that we're sitting next to each other on the same side of the table. It would just be normal and we would know and everyone else would know that we're a couple who does business together. See what I mean?"

She stares at me in silence for what feels like a long time.

"What?" I ask. "It's fine with me if you do want to put it on ice. I just need to know. I can't keep living with all these questions and confusion."

She gulps and her face turns white. "You said you wanted a relationship."

"I do want a relationship. Isn't that what we talked about before? I told you I want everything."

"So....you don't want to put it on ice?" she asks. "Because I'm fine with that, too, if that's what you need to keep your life on track."

"No!" I can't help but lean across the table and take her hand. "I don't want that. I want you. I want all of what we have and more. I want you all the time."

She gazes back into my eyes with so much poignant longing. Her voice cracks and she barely chokes out, "I want that, too."

"You want me all the time?" I can barely speak above a whisper. "Do you want me in my house and in my bed all the time—forever?"

She nods in pained anguish. She really does want that. I see it now. I squeeze her hand tighter. I can't let go of her. Now I really can't do more than whisper, "Don't let go of me, baby."

"I can't!" She chokes and tears spring to her eyes. "I need you, Kevin!"

"God, I need you so bad, baby!" My throat hurts from the look in her eyes. She looks so miserable without me. "You're mine! Do you hear me? You'll always be mine."

She just nods and two tears streak down her cheeks. The waiter comes back just then and she has to pull herself together so we can order.

I let go of her hand as long as he's here, but I put my hand across the table to take hers the instant he leaves. She doesn't let go, thank God.

I can't say anything else. I just want to sit here and feel how much she needs me. She needs me as much as I need her. I really want to hold her right now, but this feeling.....this is enough for right now—knowing we're together.

I don't know how it will work with her moving in with me and everything that will happen after that, but it will happen. I can live with this now. I don't have to dwell on it or wonder if she needs me as much as I need her.

I wait a long time before I break the silence. I wait until the waiter brings our food and we start eating. We can't hold hands now, but that's okay.

"I'm sorry," I murmur. "I'm sorry if I'm doing this all wrong. I've never done anything like this before."

"You're all I've ever wanted, Kevin," she croaks. "I never thought I would ever find a man like you. I want you and I also want to be like you."

"Stop it," I counter. "You're inspiring to me. You're inspiring to everyone around you—and not just because of your work. You're perfect the way you are. I've never felt this way about anyone. I've never found anyone I wanted to build a life with the way I want to build one with you."

"Me, too!" She starts to get emotional again and pulls it back by waving it away. "I always thought this life was totally beyond me and out of reach, but you make it so effortless and comfortable. I don't want to go out looking for something else when I already have something as perfect as this right in front of me."

I find myself smiling at her. "I really want to take you home right now."

She makes a face and winds up blushing. "Maybe wait until after work today."

I take a chance and put my hand across the table. She takes it. "We're going to start living a normal life together where you go to your work and I go to mine. Then we'll come back together in the evening and work around each other's schedules so we can build a routine that's sustainable long-term."

She nods. "That's what I want, too."

"Are you happy at my place?" I ask.

"I love your place. I've never imagined anything like it—but it's so warm and welcoming and comfortable—like you."

I laugh. "I guess I kinda rubbed off on the place."

She squeezes my hand. "I love that about you."

I try to look away and fail. "You're beautiful. Everything about you is beautiful, especially your precious heart. I want that heart to myself."

"You have it!" she chokes. "You should know that by now."

Chapter 26: Kevin

Paige and I get through the rest of lunch. I don't want to leave. "Can I pick you up after work?" I ask.

She nods and opens her mouth to answer, but her phone rings right then. She turns aside to answer it. She frowns at the screen. "Unknown number. I wonder who it is."

She answers and her face turns white. "Uh....okay......I'm on my way. I'm coming right now. Thank you for calling me. I'll be right there." She hangs up.

"What's going on?"

"Trent is in the hospital. He was on his way to the airport to leave town the way he said he was going to and he got hit by a car. He's in the emergency department and I'm his emergency contact." She grabs her purse and stands up. "I'm really sorry. I gotta go."

"I'll come with you. You'll need someone in your corner in case he tries to attack,"

She snorts, but she's already hustling out of the restaurant too fast. I pay the bill as quickly as possible and find her on the curb outside trying to flag a cab. None of them stop for her.

"Damn it," she mutters "I walked here from the building. I don't have a car lined up."

"Let me drive you. Come on." I take her arm in one hand and pull out my phone with the other to call Rashid.

He picks us up at the next corner. I hold her hand on the way to the hospital, but I don't talk to her or try to take her mind off the situation. She keeps her lips clamped shut and stares out the opposite window.

Rashid drops us off at the emergency department entrance and drives off to find a place to park. Paige and I go inside and consult the nurse at the triage desk.

She points down the hall. "He's down there, last bed on the left."

"How bad is it?" Paige's voice trembles. "Is he....is he in danger?"

The nurse gives us a sour look. "No, he isn't in danger. He has a broken arm and a concussion. The doctors just came through here and ordered his discharge paperwork. He should be getting out in an hour at the most."

Paige blinks at her for a second trying to take it all in. Then Paige turns around in a daze. She doesn't seem to register anything that's going on around her. She must have really thought Trent was dying.

I lead her down the hall to the last bed on the left. A curtain surrounds it so Trent doesn't see that I'm here. That's the last thing any of us needs.

I stop Paige a few beds down from him, turn her to face me, and cup her cheeks so she has to look me in the eye. "I'll wait out here, okay?" I murmur, "I'll listen and make sure he doesn't do anything. Understand? I'll be right here if you need me."

She nods in shock. I almost don't want to let her go in there to talk to him. She's in no condition to deal with him considering everything he's put her through.

I guess I don't have a choice about that. She has to deal with him one way or the other. I kiss her on the forehead, let her go, and she disappears behind the curtain. I stand close enough to hear their conversation.

"Oh, you came!" he moans.

"Yeah, I came. The nurse just told me you're gonna be fine. The doctors are getting ready to release you."

"I couldn't stop thinking about you," he goes on. "I thought I was going to die and you were the only thing I could think of. I had to see you again. What we had—it was all I've ever wanted."

Her tone goes hard in an instant. "I might be your emergency contact, Trent, but that doesn't mean we're getting back together. I'm sorry you got hurt, but we will never be together again. Get that through your head."

A different nurse comes by just then and goes behind the curtain to check something. She must be getting ready to release him because she leaves the curtain mostly open. I can see Paige and Trent in there, but he doesn't notice me standing outside.

"Come on, baby," he wheedles. "We can work this out. We're married, aren't we? That means sticking together and working through our differences. Don't push me away."

"Working through our differences? Is that what you call it?" Paige snaps. "You better leave for the airport as soon as you get out of the hospital, Trent. Get on a plane and fly back to North Carolina where you belong. That's what you originally planned to do, so you better do it."

The nurse gives Paige a hard look. "You might show a little compassion. He's injured and lying in a hospital bed. At least be a decent human being about it."

"Compassion?" Paige fires back. "We just got divorced—because he dumped me. He did this—not me—and then he went and screwed four women at the same time in our bed the very next night after he told me it was over. I'm not his emergency contact anymore, so if anything happens to him, you can call someone else—not me." She turns back to Trent. "Don't ever contact me again, Trent—for any reason. We're done."

She storms out so fast that she accidentally crashes into me before she realizes I'm standing so close. I grab her to steady her. "Easy!" I murmur. "Take it easy. It's over. Come on. I'll drive you home."

I take her outside and put her in the limo. She's as shaken up now as she was when she first got the phone call. What a scumbag Trent is to use his injury to come crawling back to her.

I get Rashid to wait outside while I lead Paige up to her apartment. It's still the middle of the workday, but she needs to take some time to calm down.

I pull her onto the couch to sit next to her. "Everything will be all right," I tell her. "He'll leave town and then he won't be your problem anymore."

"He isn't my problem now!" she snaps, but I still hear her voice shaking. "He's a dipshit for telling the hospital staff to call me. He's a loser."

"You're right. You don't need someone like that in your life." I kiss the side of her head. "Do you want me to stick around and keep you company? I don't think you should go back to work until you calm down."

She casts her eyes at her hands in her lap. "I need to ask you something."

"Go ahead. You can ask me anything."

"It doesn't mean anything.....you bringing me back here....does it?"

I have to put my arms around her. She's beyond precious. "It doesn't mean anything except that we're just starting out. Would you rather I took you to my place? I didn't think you would want to move in after only our first date."

She shrugs. "It doesn't matter as long as I know we're still together."

"That's exactly how I feel." I cup her chin and lift her lips to mine for just one soft kiss. "Everything will happen for us the way we want it to. I'm certain of it. We'll just keep going until we can't go anymore. Okay? Just take some time until you're ready to go back to work. I'll text you later, okay? Maybe we can start texting and calling each other all the time. That would make both of us understand that we really are together. Then we don't have to spend days apart wondering if the other person still feels the same way."

She nods, but she doesn't smile yet. That's okay. "I would really like that."

I kiss her once more and stand up. I don't want to get stuck here. "I'll call you later and find out how you're doing. You can come over to my place if you really want to. I won't fight you off."

She finally smiles and I let myself out of the apartment. I don't want to leave her alone, but I guess we aren't there yet.

We will be, though. We're going there one way or the other.

Chapter 27: Paige

The elevator doors open in Kevin's apartment and I collapse on the couch. "I'm exhausted!" I exclaim. "We had a disaster on the production floor. It was like someone released a gremlin into the building. All the equipment broke down at the same time."

"All of it?" Kevin asks from his chair across the room. "That doesn't seem possible."

"Okay, maybe not all of it, but enough of it. Ten machines broke down all at the same time. We didn't have enough maintenance people to fix them all at once. Our plant manager called in a private engineering firm to help out the maintenance crew and the new guys completely botched it up even worse than it was before. We ended up getting rid of them all and just using our own guys. We can't trust outsiders to understand our equipment well enough."

"Wow, that sounds dramatic," he remarks.

"It was! Two of the production managers had meltdowns right in front of the crews. One of the guys started hyperventilating and thought he was having a heart attack. He told his workers to call an ambulance and then got belligerent when the medics told him there was nothing wrong with him."

Kevin bursts out laughing. "Poor guy."

"So now we're on a production delay with our first shipment of product on the new bid-offer system."

He looks up. "Is that going to be a problem for us?"

"No, no! Nothing like that. We padded out our timeframe to give us extra time to deal with unforeseen circumstances like this."

"Smart," he remarks. "In that case, maybe you'd like to go out to dinner with me."

Now I'm the one who looks up. I've been staying here every night for a week, but we still aren't calling it officially living together.

I still have my own apartment and I keep all my stuff there. I usually go home each morning to take a shower, change my clothes, and then leave for work.

"Are you sure you want to go out?" I ask. "We could cook something here."

"I'm sure I want to go out. My question is if *you* want to go out. I'll be happy to stay in if you're too exhausted to be seen in public with me."

Now I'm the one who laughs. "What woman in her right mind could refuse an invitation like that?"

He puts down his phone and comes over to kiss me. He doesn't stop until he pushes me all the way back on the couch and lowers himself on top of me. He spirals his hips into me the way he knows I love him t

ii

"I'm sure I could pump you full of all the energy you would ever need," he growls. "But then you would crash at dinner and I would have to carry you home."

"Aw!" I wrap my arms around his neck. "You're so sweet."

He stands up. "Come on. Let's go out."

He takes me upstairs and we both get dressed in our finest. I love going out with him. He always treats me like a lady. Walking around on his arm feels wonderful and gives me so much confidence.

We exchange smirks back and forth across the seat in the back of the limo. Riding in the limo with him turns me on. It reminds me of all the things he could do to me in the back of the limo.

He never does them, though. That's what's so exciting and erotic about it. We're both thinking it and we both know we'll do all of that once we get back home. The limo represents the anticipation and desire that comes before the main event.

He takes me to an upscale restaurant in the east Forties. The restaurant is in the basement of a big skyrise office tower, but the restaurant is luxurious, quiet, and elegant.

Kevin gets us a booth in a shadowy corner where we can make a whole lot of eye contact across the candlelit table.

He takes my hand and gazes at me across the table. His eyes glow with so much depth and warm admiration. "This last week has been a dream come true for me," he murmurs. "It's everything I hoped it would be and more."

"It's such a relief, isn't it? It's such a relief when I'm at work and everything is going wrong to know that I'm going to go home to you at the end of the day and everything will be okay. It makes it so much easier to deal with everything."

He squeezes my hand. "I feel the same way. How are you feeling about what we talked about?"

"Which part?" I laugh. "We talk about a lot of things."

"I mean the part about you staying at my place all the time—forever. Do you remember that conversation?"

I feel my cheeks burning. "Yes, I remember."

"So how are you feeling about it?"

"I feel the same way I did then. My feelings for you haven't changed. If anything, this past week has only confirmed that it really is what we both want." I frown at him. "Has it confirmed that it really is what you want? Do you feel the same way?"

"Yes, absolutely. I just wanted to make sure we were still on the same page about that."

"It sounds like we are. I don't see how anything could change—except maybe that I would move my clothes into your closet and my toothbrush into your bathroom. It would just mean I didn't have to go home every morning—which would give us more time together."

"How do you feel about that?"

I shrug. "I'm ready whenever you are. I don't see how that could ever change—not by much, anyway."

He falls silent for a minute and the waiter comes just then to take our order. Kevin and I both tell him what we want and he leaves.

Kevin waits just long enough until we're alone before he slides around the booth to sit right next to me. He puts his arm around my shoulders and looks straight down into my eyes.

"I can think of one thing that would change—at least, I want it to," he murmurs. "It would be slightly different than you moving your clothes into my closet and your toothbrush into my bathroom. I don't know. Maybe you aren't interested, though."

I look up at him. "What do you mean? How would it change?"

He takes a small, grey velvet ring box out of his pocket and puts it on the table in front of me. "Open it," he tells me.

I stare down at the box. I can't believe I'm looking at this. We've barely been going out for more than a few weeks.

We've known each other a lot longer than that. I've known him for a long time. I've known him in business. I've known him personally. I've known him through some of the most difficult times of my life.

"I meant it when I said forever," he murmurs in my ear. "I don't want you to move your stuff into my apartment—not unless you're really going to be mine, body and soul, forever. I want you all to myself. I want to know you're mine. I don't want to half-ass this or leave you in any doubt about my intentions. I want it all—including the gold ri ng."

I can't even look up at him. The box mesmerizes me into a trance. He's really saying that. He's.....proposing.

"I've known since that first night," he goes on. "I guess that's why I got so confused. I didn't want to scare you by telling you how I felt, but it just keeps getting stronger and I get more certain every day that I want you. I want you always and forever in every possible way. I won't be satisfied with anything less."

Those words ring in my head with a kind of fatal certainty. I knew that first night, too. I just didn't want to admit it—to myself or to him. I didn't want him to think I was moving too fast.

"Do you want to put it on?" he breathes.

I nod down at the box. I can't think. He isn't doing this—but he is. He wants to marry me.

He opens the box and sets it back in the same place so I can see the large emerald-cut diamond sitting in a setting of white gold and small-er stones running down the sides. The ring is exquisite and gleams with a subtle pale pink color.

"Do you like it?" he asks.

I can only nod. *Like* isn't the word I would use to describe this ring. It looks like something royalty would wear. I don't dare to touch it.

He pulls it out and slips it on my finger. I keep staring at the ring even after he puts it on my hand. I can't believe it.

He gets my attention by raising my knuckles to his lips and then cupping my chin to raise my face. Our eyes meet.

"I love you," he murmurs. "I've never loved anyone like this before. You have my heart more than I ever thought it was possible for anyone to have it. I want yours in return. Being with you has made me happier than I ever thought I could be. I never want to live without you again."

I wrap my arms around his neck and hug him tight. I clamp my eyes shut in the whirlwind tempest of emotions coursing through me right now.

I don't have to hide how I feel about him. I don't have to hide it from him. I don't have to make him think I want to take it slowly or that I'm in any doubt about what this means.

I don't want to live without him, either. I don't want to keep going home to my own apartment, not even to take a shower every morning and change my clothes. I don't want to do any of it anymore.

I just want to go home with him and stay there always—in his house and in his bed the way we talked about. That's where I belong. I don't belong anywhere else.

We pull apart and he slides over to his side of the table. We hold hands until the waiter brings our food.

The ring glimmers on my finger every time I move. The ring feels strange. It wasn't that long ago when I wore Trent's ring on that finger.

This feels lightyears different from that. The ring casts a different energy over me. I'm Kevin's now. I'm his and he can call me his. That feeling makes me into a different person than I was just a few minutes ago.

We eat our food in silence, but only for a little while.

"Can I ask you a question?" he asks.

"Of course. My middle name is Sabrina, by the way."

He laughs. "Mine is Walter. Don't laugh."

I burst out laughing before I have a chance to stop myself. "I'm sorry. It's a nice name."

"No, it isn't. Don't lie."

I try not to choke on my food and wind up doing it anyway.

"I wanted to ask you about the deal you had with Trent where you kept your money separate," he goes on.

"Yeah. What about it?"

"How do you feel about that now? Do you want to do the whole pre-nup thing the way you did before—and keep all your assets separate and everything? How do you feel about it now? Do you have any regrets or would you do it the same way the second time around?"

I cock my head to study him, and at that moment, his eyes dart sideways and all the light goes out of his face. I follow his gaze and my stomach plummets.

We both watch a couple leave the restaurant at that moment. The man pauses to hold the door open for the woman—and the man glances back toward the booth where Kevin and I sit talking.

The man is Emerson Sinclair, son of Montgomery Sinclair, Diego Espinosa's business partner. There's no question about it. Emerson definitely saw me and Kevin together.

I stare after Emerson when he disappears up the stairs to leave the restaurant. I don't know if Emerson saw Kevin sitting next to me and proposing to me, but Emerson definitely saw enough.

Word will probably get back to Montgomery and then to Diego about me and Kevin going out together. Word will probably get back to The Billionaires' Club about it.

I turn around and face Kevin. It's already too late to stop it from happening. The information is out there. I'm not going to run Emerson down and beg him or bribe him or threaten him not to tell anyone that Kevin and I are together.

I'm wearing his ring on my finger. Everyone is going to find out pretty soon—and I want them to. I'm proud to be with him. Any woman would be.

He glances at me and goes back to eating. "Nothing to worry about," he tells me.

I nod. "Where were we?"

"You were about to tell me about whether you wanted to keep your finances separate from mine."

I study him for a minute, but I don't even have to do that. I already know the answer.

"I don't think it's necessary and I don't want to," I tell him. "I don't want to give myself an out clause on our relationship. If we're going in, I want to go all in. It isn't as though you have a reason to go after my money and I have no reason to go after yours."

He nods. "I feel the same way. I want to invest all my confidence in you."

"Maybe we should look into some kind of legal structure that puts our assets in trust...you know....." I stop myself again.

His eyes go hard. "Go on and say it. We're both already thinking it."

I gulp. "Are you sure?"

"I definitely am. If you're thinking it, you might as well say it. Get it all out on the table. Why hold back if that's what we both want?"

I hesitate —but only until I see the ring on my finger. What would this ring mean if not that?

"I was going to suggest that we put our assets into a trust for future generations—in case we have any."

He bursts out in a huge smile. "I want that. Do you?"

"Yes. I always have."

He clasps my hand. "Then let's look into it. Then neither of us has to worry about the other one cutting us off because everything we have will already be going to them."

I beam at him across the table. "That sounds perfect. I love that."

He flags the waiter. "Let's get out of here. I want to take you home so I can tear that dress off you."

I giggle. "You'll have to catch me first."

"You're mine now, remember?"

"How could I forget?"

Chapter 28: Kevin

I walk into The Billionaires' Club and find Lane and Judah already there waiting for me. "You fellas are early," I tell them. "What's the occasion?"

"You aren't the only one who can be early," Judah tells me. "Some of us can be punctual when we absolutely have to be."

"This isn't punctual. This is obsessed."

"And that's why *you're* here, isn't it?" Lane adds. "You always come early."

"Jackson says you've been taking on the finance officer's job," Judah goes on. "Do we need to have a conversation about that?"

"You don't have to because he already did—and I don't have to tell you what having a conversation with Jackson is like." I raise my right hand. "I swear I won't do it again."

"Then why are you here so early?" Lane asks. "Are you sneaking glances at the bills behind his back?"

"Why are *you* here so early?" I ask. "You're going to start making me look bad."

We all laugh and the other guys come in a few minutes later.

"Let's get started with our first agenda item," Dante begins, "We have two new applicants and three events coming up. Let's assign organizing committees for the events and....."

"Just a minute, Dante," Rory interrupts. "I have an agenda item I want to raise. I think we should address it first because it affects the whole club."

Dante looks up. "What is it?"

Rory turns to me. "Diego says that Emerson Sinclair saw you out on a date with Paige. Emerson says it looks like you two are involved."

"We are involved," I tell him. "We've been involved for a while."

"Don't you think that's a little inappropriate?" he asks. "You're the membership officer and she's a new member."

"She isn't a new member. She's been a member for months and no one can accuse me of making a move on her during the application process. This would be the same as any member getting involved with any other member. There's no rule against that."

"I'm bringing this up as the club's PR officer," Rory goes on. "The press is going to find out about this if they haven't already. It would look really bad if the person responsible for orienting new members used his position to work his way into the life of one of the very few female billionaires to join this club."

"I didn't use my position for that." I try to keep the irritation out of my voice, but it creeps in anyway. "She was married when she first showed up here and I treated her the same way I treat everyone else. I have nothing to apologize for and I'm not going to apologize."

"Just explain to us how it happened," Jackson tells me. "How did you get involved with her? We all saw the chemistry between you when she first showed up here."

I raise both hands. "I'm not going to debate whether there was chemistry between us or not, but I would challenge anyone here or anyone in the club or anyone who works with her or anyone who knows her at all to find any example of her behavior toward me that was any different from the way she treats everyone else. She was just as bubbly and friendly and engaging with me as she was with Diego and everyone else—and that includes every one of you standing here right now."

None of them says anything because they all know I'm right.

"I would also challenge anyone of you to find any example of *my* behavior that was any different from how I treat everyone else," I go on. "I treated her exactly the same way I would have treated any male applicant. I would never make any kind of suggestion like that to a new applicant no matter how attractive I found her—and she told us that very first day that she was married. I didn't need to hear anything else. I treated her, her husband, and her marriage with the utmost respect. I never did anything with her until after her divorce was final—and even then, she was the one who made the first move. I actively discouraged her and distanced myself from her until then. That's when we got involved and I have no plans to back down from this relationship. You can call her in to confirm everything I'm saying. I'm not going to admit any wrongdoing."

Rory turns to the others. "I think we should meet separately to decide what to do about this."

"There is nothing for you to decide and you won't be able to do anything because I haven't done anything wrong," I tell him. "I would step down as membership officer or even quit the club entirely over this. This relationship is more important to me. I'm going to marry her and the club doesn't have the power to regulate the members' personal relationships anyway. Each of you got involved with your wives under unusual circumstances. This is ours. Get used to it. We're together and that's the way it's going to stay."

"I agree with you," Judah replied. "No one here has any foundation to judge you for getting together with her however it happened—and we all know your character well enough not to question it. I believe you when you say you waited until after her divorce was final."

"I believe you, too," Rory adds. "I'm just concerned about how this is going to look when it comes out in the press. She's been divorced for less than two months and the press is already looking for a million reasons to point the finger at us."

"They're going to do that anyway," Dante points out. "The press had kittens when I married Emberlynn. Don't you remember? They made it out like I was being predatory by going after some young, innocent, impressionable underage girl who couldn't make decisions for herself."

"The same thing happened when the press found out I was marrying the woman who used to be my assistant," Jackson adds. "They made it out that I used my power and threatened her employment if she didn't get involved with me."

"I agree with Kevin that the club doesn't have the power to make any decisions about a member's personal lives," Lane chimes in. "Judah, Jackson, and Dante were all officers in the club when they got together with their wives. None of us called them on the carpet to explain and defend their actions. We all know and trust Kevin. I can't think of anyone better to be our membership officer and continue to be responsible for welcoming our new members. He's been fulfilling that role for years and inducted plenty of female billionaires into our membership. He hasn't expressed any interest or made any of them even slightly uncomfortable. He obviously has something special with Paige and we all saw that he conducted himself perfectly the whole time she was married to Trent. I say we put this matter aside and leave it alone."

"Thank you, Lane," I murmur.

"Are you okay with that, Rory?" Dante asks. "We don't want any lingering resentments or suspicions."

"No, not at all. I just thought I should bring it up because Diego raised a concern about how it would affect the club's public image."

"I say we treat this exactly the way we've treated every other nonexistent scandal the press wants to bring up in relation to the club," Judah replies. "Kevin has explained the matter to our satisfaction. We've considered the club's position and decided that we can't find any fault with his conduct or his involvement with Paige. We've therefore chosen to act accordingly and put the matter to rest. End of story. You can tell the press that."

Rory glances at me and nods. "All right. I can do that."

"And you're okay with that?" I ask. "Don't say that to my face and then keep thinking it behind my back."

"I wouldn't do that," he insists. "That's exactly why I brought it up—so the club could decide how to address it if it needed to be addressed."

"We've made the decision. This matter is now closed." Dante holds out his hand to me. "Congratulations, by the way. You're one lucky dog."

"I'll say!" Jackson exclaims. "Paige is an angel."

I feel my cheeks burning. "Thank you. I couldn't be happier."

"So when's the big day?" Lane asks. "Where are you having it?"

"We haven't actually discussed that. Actually....." I falter. "Actually, I was waiting to hear when the dates for the next series of galas will be. I was going to ask her if she wants to turn one of the galas into a wedding."

The guys fall all over themselves gasping and exclaiming.

"No way!" Jackson chokes.

Dante laughs and claps me on the shoulder. "This is perfect! It's going to be sensational."

"Now I'm really jealous," Jackson adds. "I should have thought of that."

"No! Your wedding was beautiful," I tell him.

"Okay!" Dante rubs his hands together. "We better get down to brass tacks and hammer out the dates for our next series of galas. Then you can check with Paige, ask her which one she likes the best, and find out what she wants. She might not even want a gala wedding. She might want something small, intimate, and understated. You better ask her."

"Okay, I will. Just give me the dates so I can offer them if she does go for it."

The guys all start talking. Rory never brings it up again that Paige and I got together in the club.

We didn't. That's the thing. We did everything right—but I wouldn't give her up even if the guys did decide to do something about it. I would burn the whole world to the ground for a chance to marry her. I won't let something like this stop me.

Chapter 29: Paige

I smirk when I walk into the People, Inc. lobby and find Kevin there waiting for me.

"Hey, good-looking," he murmurs. Then he slips his arm around me and kisses me right there in front of the receptionist and everything.

I turn pink, kiss him back, and squirm out of his arms. "Keep it clean."

"I am. You're wearing my ring. I can kiss you in the lobby. It isn't like I'm groping you or anything."

I laugh, head for the elevator, and we get in together. "So what did you want to show me?"

"The military is sending over their first batch of personnel for training next week. A bunch of inspectors from the Department of Defense showed up yesterday and demanded to inspect the equipment to find out how it works. They demanded specs on the equipment, design drafts, instruction manuals—the works. They say they won't let their people train on the equipment unless and until we let these inspectors study, understand, and yes, even copy the literature on your machines."

I spin around and gape at him. "They can't do that! Our designs are all patented and proprietary."

"I know. That's what I wanted to show you."

He leads me down a hallway between a bunch of different classrooms. Civilian trainees from People, Inc. occupy the rooms getting lectured by the new batch of trainers who just completed the People, Inc. trainer training program. None of these people are military.

Kevin stops at an unmarked door and uses his code card to unlock it. He swings the door back to reveal all the equipment Mike sent over for the trainers to use in their courses.

I stare at the equipment all stacked one machine on top of the other. Then I glance behind me toward the classrooms. The trainers are doing book work at the moment. None of the new trainees has gotten to the practical, hands-on, clinical part of the courses.

"We locked all the equipment in here for safekeeping," Kevin murmurs in my ear. "We'll keep it locked up until we can make sure your copyright is protected. We might need to take steps to stop the military guys from interfering when our new trainees start their practical modules."

My head jerks up. "What do you mean?"

He waves me farther down the hall and stops me before we get to the last classroom. My blood runs cold when I see five officers standing inside. They all wear fatigues.

"They refuse to leave until we give them the access they want," Kevin goes on. "They're claiming we're violating our contract by withholding vital information that could pose a national security risk to the rest of the country and US interests abroad." He makes a face at me when he says it.

"That's ludicrous, Kevin!" I counter. "They want to copy my design! That's what this is! They want all that information so they can build their own, rip off my design, and cut SigmaTech out of the process! That's all this is!"

"I know," he murmurs. "That's why we locked up all the equipment. I want you to take all this equipment back to SigmaTech and get it out of the building as soon as possible. I might even go as far as to suggest that we wait until after business hours when these officers leave to go home for the night. Then we can bring in a crew to remove the equipment so the military doesn't have access to it anymore. We can straighten out our contractual disagreement after that when your equipment and your paperwork aren't in danger anymore."

I pass my hand across my eyes. "I don't believe I'm hearing this."

"We'll just go ahead with our civilian contracts and continue taking bids from customers on our waiting list."

"How will you deal with it once the trainees do get to the practical modules?" I ask.

"We'll set up at another venue. Do you remember when I told you I was thinking about opening other branches? We were thinking of opening our first new branches in the other boroughs. We can announce it privately just to these classes that we're holding our practical sessions in our other premises and offer to bus the trainees there for the day. It's a stop-gap measure just until we straighten out this crap with the military."

"And if we can't straighten it out?" I groan. "I don't even want to think about it."

"Then we go to court to stop them from violating your copyright. We sue the shit out of the US government for industrial espionage, make them look terrible, and include it as a condition of their settlement that they cancel our contract. We walk away, we stick to our civilian customers, and the US military loses out on all that technology. It isn't like real patients are missing out. It's the US military, for Christ's sake. It isn't a humanitarian organization. We aren't going to play games with your hard-earned designs. Hell no."

I let out a shaky breath. "Okay. Thank you for going to bat for our interests. That means a lot."

He puts his arm behind my back. "I'll walk you out and then I'll organize for some of my trucker recruits to drive all this stuff back to SigmaTech in a rented moving van after hours. These military guys will never have to know that closet is empty. They can keep believing we have the equipment on the premises and the government can continue to waste taxpayer dollars keeping these jokers on the clock waiting for us to unlock the door."

I laugh, but my heart isn't in it. "Thank you."

We get into the elevator and he kisses me again there. "I would have manufactured a reason to get you over here one way or the other. I missed you."

"You missed me just since this morning?"

"I always miss you."

The elevator doors open in the lobby. "I guess I have to go back to work now—and so do you." My phone rings in my purse just then. I barely glance at the screen. "That's strange."

"What is?"

"The call is from my sister. She hasn't spoken to me since my nephew died. I wonder why she's calling me now."

"You better answer it," he tells me.

I answer the phone "Hello?"

"Dad just died," my sister Tanya tells me. "He died of kidney failure and passed away in his bed. The funeral is on Saturday."

She hangs up on me without giving me a chance to say a word. I stare at the phone in my hand. It doesn't seem to belong to me anymore.

"What's wrong, baby?" Kevin asks.

"My dad just died." Those words come from somewhere far away from me. "The funeral is on Saturday."

"We better get you to the airport." He puts his arm around me again and takes out his phone. "I'll call Rashid to come and get us....."

I jolt back to my senses and turn around to touch his jacket. "No, Kevin! You have to stay here. You have to keep our other contracts going and I need you to handle this whole military thing for me. I have to go.....and I have to go alone. Please. I need to know someone I trust is here handling things in my absence."

His features soften. "Okay, baby. I understand. I got it. You don't have to worry about anything."

I kiss him. "Thank you. I'm really sorry to dump this on you."

"Don't apologize." His features pinch. "Just.....just come back to me."

"Always. I'll call you tonight when I get there."

I rush out of the lobby. I can't stand the look in his eyes. He's a lot more concerned about how I'll handle going home to North Carolina and dealing with my family. He doesn't know if I'll come back or if our relationship will go back to what it was.

He's wondering how it will be for me being around Trent and all my old friends and relatives. He's wondering if anything will convince me to leave all of this behind and stay there.

I can't think about any of that. I rush to the curb, flag a cab to my apartment, pack an overnight bag with the bare essentials, and rush away to the airport to catch the first flight out of town.

Chapter 30:
Paige

I draw in an unsteady breath when I get off the plane at Raleigh-Durham Airport. I had actually started to convince myself that I wouldn't have to come back to North Carolina...like ever.

Now I am back. I can just imagine the welcome waiting for me when I get to my hometown. I don't know if Trent ever actually left New York, but if he did, he'll be here, too. I can't wait.

I have to rent a car and drive out to my hometown of Henderson in the far northern part of the state. The drive is really nice. I actually love this place. I just don't always get along with the people.

I pull into town and get a rush of old memories on my way down the street. Almost every building holds some memory or another.

I drive a little farther out of town to my dad's house—the house I grew up in. The house is deserted. No one else is around. I dread what I'll find when I walk in, but I don't find anything or anyone.

The place doesn't feel like anyone has lived here in years. My dad lived here alone after all of us kids moved away. My mom died more than twelve years ago.

All my dad's possessions are in exactly the same places. No one has touched them. It doesn't look like anyone has set foot in the house since he died. That on its own is odd. My sister, Tanya, her husband, and their two children live right here in town.

My older brother Nick lives in Omaha with his family. I don't know if they'll come to the funeral. I don't even know if Tanya called him to tell Nick that our dad is dead.

I take a chance and call Tanya back. She answers with her usual brisk, businesslike tone. "Hello?"

"I'm at Dad's house. I just got into town. What do you want to do with the house and all of Dad's stuff? You and Nick and I should get together and decide what we want to keep and if any of you wants to keep the house."

"Nick doesn't want any of Dad's stuff and neither do I," she practically snaps. Her tone tells me loud and clear exactly how this is going to go. "You can get rid of it."

"You want me to get rid of it—all of it?" I ask. "Aren't you and Nick going to help out at all?"

"Nick is only coming into town for a few hours for the funeral on Saturday. Then he's flying out. I don't want anything from the house. Just take what you want and get rid of the rest."

I cringe. This is so much worse than I expected.

I don't know what I expected. Maybe I thought my dad's death would somehow bring us all together and we could all just magically forgive the hurt of the past. I thought wrong.

"What do you want to do with the house?" I ask.

"Sell it," she counters. "Do whatever you want with it."

"Dad didn't leave the house only to me, Tanya. I'm certain he didn't."

"Then sell it and divide the money. I don't care."

"So you don't even want to be involved in selling it or deciding how we sell it or how much to sell it for? You don't want to do anything?"

"I'm sure you can handle all of that since you know better than everyone else."

I clamp my eyes shut—and my mouth. So she's bringing up all of that again. I should have known. Don't ask me why I was so naïve as to expect anything different.

Part of me wants to scream at her that I only ever tried to help her family and that I never made it out that I know better than anyone else about anything.

My mind switches in that moment. She doesn't want to deal with me and neither does Nick. They're both dumping this on me = to handle all by myself.

In a way, they're doing me a massive favor. I really don't want to deal with them, either. I wouldn't be here at all if not for my dad's death.

I've been living the life of my dreams back in New York, living in luxury apartments, socializing with billionaires, and going out with the nicest guy on the planet. I'm wearing his engagement ring on my finger right now.

In a way, Nick and Tanya are solving a huge problem for me. I would have felt extremely conflicted about marrying Kevin without at least inviting my surviving siblings and their families to the wedding.

I don't have to worry about that anymore. I don't have to worry about any of this. I don't have to talk to anyone. I don't have to consult with anyone.

I don't have to deal with any of that nonsense ever again. Tanya is giving me a pass. This could actually be the best thing that's ever happened to me. It frees me from holding onto a past that doesn't benefit me anymore.

"Okay," I tell her. "I can do that."

She hangs up on me without another word. That's it. That's the end of my relationship with my only sister. I can expect something similar to happen with Nick and that's okay. It just means I'll get back to New York faster.

I go back into the house and start going through the place one room at a time. Most of the stuff in here isn't worth keeping. The furniture is all ancient and threadbare just like the soft furnishings.

My dad's clothes are old, moth-ridden, and his old personal papers are yellowed with age and covered in illegible chicken scratch. He has a bunch of old books that someone might be interested in. I might even be interested in taking one or two home with me.

I make a few quick decisions, call a realtor to come out and list the house, and order a dumpster to throw away most of this stuff. Then I drive into town to buy a bunch of boxes from the hardware store.

I cruise the aisles until I find the boxes. I'm just deciding what size to get when two people pass me in the next aisle. They give me a dirty look across the shelf between us. "Tramp!" the woman hisses.

I look up and my eyes fall out of their sockets. Trent's parents, Marlene and Damen Novak, stand there glaring at me like I'm the worst criminal alive.

I open my mouth to protest my innocence, but Marlene cuts me off. "Trent told us all about what you did, you worthless piece of meat," she snarls. "That man gave you everything and you threw it back in his face! You turned your back on him when he was in the emergency room with life-threatening injuries! I knew you were bad news the minute I laid eyes on you."

My anger dies instantly. "Trent has obviously been telling you a bunch of stories that aren't true." I pull out my phone and show her the footage of Trent and his women in our bed. "This is what your son was up to in New York before *he* divorced *me*. Now do you understand?"

Marlene shuts her mouth real quick when she sees the footage. Damen turns away and they both leave the store without another word to me. No one else better decide to pick a fight with me.

Trent has some nerve coming back here and spreading lies around when he was the dirtbag who ruined our marriage.

None of that matters because all of this is just another reason for me to get the hell out of Henderson and never come back.

I buy my boxes and motor back to my dad's house. I have a lot of work to do and not a lot of time to do it. I want to get this done so I can get on the first plane back to New York after the funeral. Nick is doing it so I can do it, too.

I get to work clearing everything out of the house room by room. I throw everything unusable and unsalvageable into a pile out front. The dumpster shows up two hours later and I start pitched everything inside.

I have to move all the furniture out by myself. I'll be damned if I call anyone to come and help me. They don't need me and I don't need them.

I can't fit the couch through the door, so I go out to the garden shed and bring in my dad's firewood axe. I turn the couch over onto its top and use the axe to hack the damn thing to smithereens.

I have to use all my strength to chop up the wooden frame. I vent all my frustration and grief onto the wood to make it shatter. I wind up bellowing out in rage—and then I burst into tears.

All the pain comes rushing back—all the pain of the past and all the pain of the present. It isn't enough that my own relatives made this town a living hell for me. Now they have to turn my dad's death into Act 2.

I collapse on my knees sobbing hard. I have nothing left—except that I do. I have my whole life waiting for me in New York. I just have to get out of here.

I call Kevin. It's seven o'clock in the evening. He's sitting on one of the couches in one of his many living rooms.

I burst into a fresh flood of tears when I see him in the apartment. I just want to be back there with him far, far away from all of this.

He doesn't say a word when the video connects and he sees me bawling my eyes out. He just sits there watching me. He's always there. He never judges or tells me to feel better.

He waits for almost twenty minutes before he murmurs. "Baby....I love you so much..."

"I can't do this, Kevin!" I howl. "I just want to go home! I just want to go home to you and the apartment and SigmaTech and everything."

"I know, baby. We'll be together very soon. I love you. I don't want to live without you here, either."

I break down crying again. He's the only person who understands because he's the only person who knows the whole truth.

I don't even have to tell him about Tanya refusing to help me. I don't have to tell him about chopping up my father's couch with an axe. I don't tell him about Marlene Novak calling me a tramp in the middle of a public hardware store.

Kevin would support me even if he knew. He probably already suspected that me coming back here would lead to something like this

I finally wipe the tears off my face. I look hideous in the camera, but he doesn't care.

"I miss you," I croak.

"I miss you, too," he breathes. "I wish I was there to help you."

I nod and bite back another grimace of despair. My family and everyone else who knows me would probably just become even more hateful if I showed up here on the arm of some hotshot billionaire with enough money to buy the whole town.

Oh, what am I saying? I am a hotshot billionaire with enough money to buy the whole town.

"When do you think you'll make it home, baby?" he asks.

"The funeral is Saturday, so as soon after that as I can get a flight. I didn't know how things would go, so I bought a changeable ticket for the following morning. I'll have to check and see if I can get something sooner. The Sunday flight isn't until noon, but I would have to drive back to Raleigh anyway."

He only nods. He doesn't ask what made me decide to fly home immediately after the funeral. I would get in the car and drive to the airport straight from the church if I thought I could get a flight that soon.

"Did you straighten out the thing with the equipment?" I ask.

He smiles through the screen and checks his watch. "The truckers are coming at midnight. I'm staying awake so I can meet them at the building, help them load up, and then travel with them to talk to the SigmaTech people on the other end. I contacted your executive team about it and they're coming in to meet me."

"What are you going to do about the contract?"

"I talked to Diego right after you left. He brokered the deal for us and he has a bunch of other pending contracts with them, so he'll put pressure on them to cave on their demands—and of course both the SigmaTech legal team and the People, Inc. legal team are already involved."

I cover my eyes. "This funeral is the last thing I need to be messing with right now."

"Just do what you have to do to take care of your business. If any of your family is worth connecting with, then connect with them and keep those connections alive. If they aren't, then just tie up any loose ends and get out of Dodge."

I nod. "That's what I plan to do. In fact, I should probably get back to that now. Thank you for everything. I love you. I'm going to come home just as soon as I can."

He smiles at me. "Call me if you need anything—around the clock. I mean it."

"I will. Don't stay up too late tonight, okay?"

"I'll try not to. I love you. I'll see you on Sunday at the latest."

We both hang up. He's all I need. I don't need any of this other bullshit.

I put my phone away and get back to work. I just get angry when I work to break up the couch. I have no more tears to shed for any of these people. I might be able to shed a few for my parents, but no one else.

I get the three bedrooms cleaned out. Nick and Tanya have both left a bunch of their old school certificates and trophies in their rooms. I don't feel right about throwing all of this away, but Tanya did tell me to just get rid of anything I didn't want.

She won't be able to come back later and blame me for this—although she did blame me for her nephew's death, so what do I know?

I pitch it all out anyway. I slow down and eventually stop when I come to family photo albums from my childhood. I don't want to throw these away—and I do want to keep them.

My dad's albums include pictures of his and my mom's families, our older relatives as children, and a bunch of other old family memorabilia.

I pack all of this in boxes to take back to New York with me. Nick and Tanya will have to contact me and actually hold a civil conversation with me if they ever want to see these pictures.

I save a bunch of my mom's old possessions, jewelry, and trinkets she kept around the house. This stuff is straight out of my childhood memories. Nick and Tanya are losing out by not keeping this stuff for themselves. That's their loss.

Slowing down makes me realize how tired I am. It's already past midnight by the time I go to my own old bedroom. A bunch of my old things are in here, too. My dad didn't clear this room out, either.

I'm too tired to face any of this right now, so I curl up on top of the bed and crash. I don't even bother to get under the covers. I don't want to get comfortable here even for one night.

Chapter 31: Paige

I get up at the crack of dawn the next morning and immediately start going through my dad's house in a whirlwind of activity. The dumpster is already half full by the time I haul every single bed and every other stick of furniture out there to throw it all away.

I'm just wiping my dusty hands on my pants after throwing away my own bed when the realtor pulls up.

"Hey!" she greets me and holds out her hand. "Paige Novak, right? You might not remember me. I'm Sandy Phelps. I used to be Sandy Turlington before I got married. We went to high school together."

"Yeah, I remember you. How you doing?"

"I'm great. How are you? I'm sorry to hear about your father."

"Thank you." I wave at the house behind me. "That's why we're selling his house."

"Sure," she tells me. "What do you want to do with it?"

"Nothing. Just sell it as quickly as possible."

"How much do you want to ask for it?"

"I have no idea and, to be totally frank with you, I really don't care. My siblings and I just want to offload it as quickly as possible, so I suppose we could put it up for auction and just take what we can get for it. How does that sound to you?"

"That's fine." She opens her folio and starts making notes. "I would send out a photographer—either today or tomorrow depending on when you want to do it."

"I don't care when we do it. I'm just cleaning the place out now—as you can see."

She grins at me. "I see that."

"So you can either photograph it now or wait until I finish. I'm leaving town over the weekend to go back to New York, so you can do it whenever you want, hold the auction whenever you want, and manage the listing however you want. I really don't care what you do as long as I don't have to come back to Henderson to complete the sale."

She frowns at me. "Are you sure? Most people don't feel this way about their childhood homes."

"I'm sure—and my siblings feel the same way. My sister Tanya lives in town. You can talk to her if you need any additional information or if you need access to the property. I'll leave you the keys before I fly out on Sunday."

She won't stop frowning. "Yeah, I know Tanya. I'm surprised she isn't more involved in this."

"Was she close to my dad?"

Her eyes shoot up. "Don't you know that?"

"Not really. Tanya hasn't spoken to me in years."

Sandy raises her hand and her eyebrows. "I don't want to know. I stay out of other people's family drama. My own is bad enough."

"Good idea. Anyway, Tanya will be your local contact after I leave town. I'll give you my phone number and email address. You should be able to conclude the sale and send me all the paperwork remotely."

"Sure, that won't be a problem."

"Is there anything you need to do? Just tell me when the photographers are going to come so I'm not in the shower or something at the time."

She laughs and I give her my contact details. She leaves and I get back to work. I'm on a mission. Nothing matters but getting the job done.

I work all day, make a bunch of trips to the secondhand store to drop stuff off, and eventually get the house somewhat passable for the photographers to show up on Friday.

I stand outside in the sunshine and check my emails while I wait for them to finish. The shit is hitting the fan back in New York. Diego is having a seizure about the military trying to steal the IP on my equipment.

He's throwing a hissy fit with the Pentagon threatening to cancel all their upcoming contracts with his suppliers if they don't back down. Good old Diego. I should have known he would see this the right way.

He's accusing them of tarnishing his reputation by manipulating him into brokering an illegal deal when they never planned to honor the contract in the first place. He's accusing them of rigging the whole process just so they could get their hands on my designs.

SigmaTech and People, Inc. don't have to sue the shit out of the government because he's planning to do it for us. He's got his own legal sharks already circling the waters waiting to pounce as soon as the military shows any sign of weakness.

I call Kevin again. We share a laugh about the whole thing, but he can't talk long because he's on his way to a Board of Directors meeting. He's pitching his idea about doing all these training projects for at-risk youth and people who want to get out of dead-end jobs.

I field a bunch of messages from my own executives and management teams. They're all over the moon about how Kevin and Diego are handling the situation.

The SigmaTech people couldn't be more thrilled to be doing business with two men who are willing to go to bat to protect someone else's company.

I put my phone back in my pocket. I can get through tomorrow's funeral knowing Kevin and Diego are on the job. I knew they were both good men. Now they're showing me just how good they really a re.

The photographers finish their work, thank me, and leave me to my cleaning. I spend the rest of Friday tossing, packing, and getting rid of everything else in the house, including the carpets. I strip the place down to the bare boards.

I have nowhere to sleep tonight, so I drive into town, ship all my boxes of memorabilia to myself in New York, and get a motel room.

I call Kevin back, but he doesn't answer his phone so I send him a text. He answers while I'm sitting in a diner down the street getting some dinner down my throat.

He bursts out laughing when he sees me. "You won't believe it, baby!" he chortles. "The Board of Directors went for it hook, line, and sinker. They loved it! They're all on board. I can't believe it! I'm on the moon!"

I can't help but smile at him. "Congratulations. You deserve this. It's gonna be great."

"I can't wait to get started! I love you so much! Thank you! Thank you a million times for giving me the idea."

"I didn't give you the idea. You thought of it all on your own."

"But you were there. You were the one who inspired it. Phew!" He bursts out in laughter again. "I gotta go! I have so much shit to do.

Oh, my God! I can't think. I need to sit down somewhere and take a bunch of notes. I need to download everything I have in my head so I can organize it."

"Okay. I'll talk to you tomorrow. I love you. Congratulations. I'm so happy for you."

He blows me a kiss through the screen and hangs up. I have to chuckle to myself. He's this excited and energetic about helping people. He's going to become a force of nature—even more than he already is. He's so wonderful—and he's all mine.

I smile down at the ring on my finger. We're engaged. I'm going home to New York to marry him.

Home. My home is with him in our apartment in New York. That's where I belong and that's where I'm going. Nothing will stop me.

I go back to my motel room and change my ticket to another flight on Saturday night. It's a red-eye, but who the hell cares? It's the first flight I can get after I drive from the funeral to the airport.

I wake up bright and early Saturday morning. The funeral isn't until one o'clock, so I have six hours to clean my dad's house.

I drive back to my motel room at eleven-thirty, take a shower, get dressed, pack my suitcase, and put it in the back of the car. I drive out to the church and park in the parking lot.

I get there at five minutes to one and the parking lot is already overflowing with cars. I have to search to find a place to park.

The church is standing room only—and I can see the minute I walk in the door that neither Tanya's family nor Nick's family has saved me a seat at the front of the church for my own father's funeral.

Every single one of these insults just adds fuel to the fire. Every slight is another reason not to stay here. I have nothing to stay for.

A bunch of people glare at me when I walk in.

"You have got some nerve showing up here, Paige," a woman snaps from my other side. I turn around and come face to face with Madeline Charleston. She's Trent's sister. Their parents, Trent, and a bunch of other members of his family are also here.

"You abandoned my brother when he was in the hospital!" Madeline goes on loud enough for the whole church to hear.

I've heard enough. I ignore the pastor standing at the pulpit, elbow past a bunch of people, plant myself in the middle of the aisle, and switch on my phone. I start playing the footage with all the screams and thumps going in the background.

"Do you see this?!" I yell out to the so-called mourners. "Do all of you see this? This is the man you're defending! He rode my coattails all the way to New York and dumped me there because I made more money than he did. He accused me with no evidence at all that I was sleeping with every man in my company—and the night after he dumped me, I came home and found this in my bed—in the apartment I paid for! He was the one who destroyed our marriage! I am the one who gave him everything and got kicked in the teeth for my trouble. He broke his arm and got a bump on his head after we had already finalized our divorce. He was on his way to the airport to leave New York when he got hurt. He wasn't critical or in a coma nor did he have any life-threatening injuries in the hospital. He was minutes away of getting discharged and he used his emergency contact to try to get me back. That's what happened—not whatever stupid story he's telling you all about how I done him wrong. I didn't owe him anything then and I don't owe him anything now after the way he treated me. Now all of you better accept that or you can get the hell out of this church! This is my father we're burying—not yours! Get out of you can't clean up your attitude. You aren't welcome here."

I turn my back on the crowd, storm to the front of the room, and jerk my thumb at some random townsperson sitting in the front pew. "Get up and move somewhere else," I snap. "I'm sitting here."

The person scampers. I turn my back to the room and face front to sit down.

I completely ignore whether anyone in Trent's family leaves the funeral. I don't give a crap about any of them or anything else. I'm here to attend my father's funeral. I don't look sideways at my own brother and sister.

The pastor waits an uncomfortable moment before he clears his throat and starts the service. I barely listen. I think about my dad. He didn't exactly support my interest in medical research and equipment, but he didn't discourage it, either.

That's saying a hell of a lot more than some people I could mention. I have no use for any of them. They don't count—not anymore. No one counts. I'm out here saving lives. To hell with anyone who has a problem with that.

My company has created thousands of jobs and will continue to save more lives and create thousands more jobs as the company grows. Anyone who has a problem with that better get behind me. I'll run them the hell over if they get in my way.

Chapter 32: Paige

My father's funeral service ends and the pastor announces that everyone is holding a picnic with refreshments outside afterward. I leave, get in my car, and drive straight to the realtor's office to drop off the keys to my dad's house. I don't ever have to go back there.

I'm on my way back to my car when my brother Nick pulls up in another rental car. He's almost as tall as Kevin. Nick has much lighter hair and he's showing the signs of age. He doesn't take care of himself the way Kevin does and it shows in both of them.

Nick comes right up to me. I stiffen for another confrontation. What does he want?

"Don't move away, Paige," he tells me. "Stay. Move back home where you belong. Don't forget where you came from."

I snort at him and turn toward my car. "I don't see you moving back to Henderson, Nick. You let me work my ass off these last three days to clean out Dad's house all on my own. You didn't come to help me and you haven't offered me a word of comfort or dignified me with a single phone call in years. You didn't even save me a seat in the front pew of the church for my own father's funeral. What were you thinking?"

"I'm sorry," he grumbles. "I've just been so messed up about this whole thing. I wasn't thinking."

"Clearly not. I have nothing to stay here for. My life is elsewhere just like yours is. I hope you and the family have a good flight back to Omaha. See you around."

I get into my car and drive off without another word of goodbye to him. I don't need to tell him how much this place disgusts and horrifies me. I would never come back here, especially not after seeing what my life could be like in New York.

I burn rubber all the way back to Raleigh. I don't stop to eat or even change my clothes. I get to the airport way too early for my flight, but I don't care. I want to get as close to New York as I possibly can as quickly as I can.

I change in the airport bathroom and get something to eat from one of the snack bars. I sit down in the waiting area outside my gate and call Kevin. It's only seven o'clock at night.

He answers lying in his bed and squints into the screen. My heart skips a beat when I see him in a pair of pajama pants with no shirt on. His hair is a mess—exactly the way I would see him if I was lying in bed with him right now.

I can't help checking him out. He's so damn hot. No one knows better than I do what it feels like to drag my hands and mouth all over that stomach, chest, and neck.

His face screws up in all the wrong ways while he pries his face out of the pillow. "Hello?" he croaks.

"I'm so sorry I woke you up. I didn't know you'd be asleep this early. I can call back later if you want me to."

"No, no." He accidentally drops his phone while he's rolling over. He curses under his breath and picks it up again.

The phone goes all wobbly while he scoots up the bed and props himself against his pillows so we can see each other. I'm looking straight down at him like we were in bed together. He is so beautiful. I love him from the bottom of my heart.

"I was just catching up on sleep after last night's clandestine Mission Impossible," he tells me.

I laugh. "Did you have to shoot your way through to get the payload out of the building?"

He grins. "Naw. No one was there. The Army guys haven't come back. I think the lawyers gave them a spanking they won't forget."

"Are you sure you don't want to go back to sleep?"

"No! I always want to hear from you no matter what time it is." He squints at the screen again. "Are you at the airport?"

"I'm catching a red-eye back to JFK. The flight doesn't get in until twelve-thirty. I'll get a car to drive me back..."

"Like hell you will! I'll come and get you. Hold on. Let me set an alarm so I wake up in time." He noodles on his phone for a minute.

"I love you," I tell him. "I can't wait to see you and to go home to our own apartment."

He looks up at the camera. "Hey, baby. I need to ask you a question."

"Go for it."

"What do you think about our wedding date? When do you want to do it?"

I shrug. "How about as soon as I get home?"

He laughs. "No! I mean it. Seriously. When do you want to get married? How long do you want to wait?"

I narrow my eyes at him. "It seems like you're asking for a specific reason. Why do you ask that?"

"Because...depending on how long you want to wait, we could get married at one of the club galas. We're having four galas this year...."

"Yes!!" I practically jump out of my seat. "Yes, I love that idea!"

He freezes in place. "Are you sure? You didn't have any other plans on how you want to get married? I don't want to rain on your parade or make it seem like I'm overruling your idea."

"No, that's great! Let's do that. When are the dates?"

"Well, like I said, we have them quarterly, so we could just plan on having the wedding at the same time as whatever gala happens to fall in that quarter."

"I really don't mind. We can do it whenever. How long were you thinking we would wait?"

"We've already planned and booked out everything for the next gala. The caterers, decorators, and servers and everything are already lined up. The next one we could turn into a wedding is in six months. Is that too soon for you?"

"Not at all. Let's do that."

He blinks at me. "Are you sure? This seems way too easy."

"No way. This is great."

"You seem much more chipper than you should be considering that your dad just died."

"I'm just really excited to get home to you and move on with the life we're going to have. I don't want to dwell in the past anymore."

"I want that, too. How about, after I pick you up at the airport, we go to your old place and you can pack up your stuff to bring it over here? Then you can stay here all the time. You don't have to go back."

"That would be wonderful. I love you. I can't wait to see you again."

He smiles for the first time. "I feel the same way. I'm going to be there at the airport—and I promise to comb my hair first." He bends close to the screen and rakes his fingers through his hair trying to get it into some kind of order.

I laugh at him. "I would love it if you showed up at the airport looking like that."

He makes a face. "Dream on, baby. You're the only person who gets to see me like this."

"I don't care what you look like as long as it's you. I better let you get back to sleep so you can see straight when you get there."

He blows me a kiss through the screen. He always does that.

We hang up and I smile to myself for the rest of the wait until I get on the flight. I don't have to wonder what will happen when I land in New York. Kevin and I will fall into each other's arms and nothing will ever come between us again.

We'll drive to my old apartment—my soon-to-be-former apartment. I'll pack the few possessions I still have there. I didn't keep much when I moved away from Trent.

I'll take all my stuff back to Kevin's apartment—our apartment. That place is my home now. I know that in the deepest marrow of my bones.

We'll start planning our gala wedding. All our friends will gather to celebrate us and our continuing success together.

I can't wait for that day—the day hovering before me in a halo of happiness. That will be the first day of the rest of my life—the first day of the rest of our lives together.

Epilogue: Kevin

I stand in the lobby of the Four Seasons Hotel. This seems to be the best place for club galas. The management and staff all know us here. We always seem to have the best galas here.

Today is the best gala ever because today is the day I'm getting married. I pace up and down waiting for Paige to show up in her limo.

She's been staying at her old apartment for the last week gearing up for the wedding. The other wives and female billionaires have been coming and going from there all week helping her get ready.

Meanwhile, I've been going crazy like a trapped beast at my apartment—our apartment. Paige and I have been living together for six months. This is the first time we've spent apart since her father's death and my nerves are at the breaking point.

I practically jump out of my skin when a limo pulls up to the hotel entrance outside. Samantha, Emberlynn, Mckenna, and Piper get out and help Paige with all her flowing skirts, veil, and train. The women carry everything behind her so none of it touches the sidewalk.

Paige looks absolutely breathtaking in a sheer white satin dress dotted with gemstones. She bursts into an equally dazzling smile when she sees me standing there in my tux.

The women go into a flurry arranging her skirts, dress, veil, and train. They lay the train out behind her so it lies the way it's supposed to. All four women shoot me big, blushing grins. I can't even get near Paige with the women in the way.

I don't want to get near her—not yet. I just want to stand here and gaze on this vision of loveliness who is my bride—the beautiful angel who is about to become my wife.

I never thought I would find her. I never thought I would find anyone like her or even remotely like her, but here she is. She's standing right in front of me all dressed up like some kind of queen ready to marry me.

Her infectious, crazy smile lights up her magnificent face. She looks so insanely happy and excited to be marrying me—even more happy and excited than she usually looks about everything.

She is such a blessing on my life. She makes my house a home. She makes my life worth living. She gives me new inspiration and new energy to keep pushing higher. I love everything about my life with h er.

The women finish straightening her out and race away into the ballroom just as the organ music switches on. I don't look in there to see what's happening because I already know.

I glide over to Paige. I'm floating on a pillow of cloud. My feet don't touch the ground. I get lost in how exquisite she looks right now—my bride.

She bursts into an even bigger, more brilliant smile when she sees me looking at her like that. Her small delicate hand slips into the crook of my arm.

I only have eyes for her as the bridal march starts to play and I escort her into the ballroom. Hundreds of people pack the place.

No one stands on any particular side. It's impossible to tell who is here for the groom and who is here for the bride—because all the guests are here for both of us and everyone.

Paige and I float up the red carpet between all the guests. Men and women stand on both sides of the hall. Every man here is my groomsman and every woman here is Paige's bridesmaid.

There would have been too many to choose from and we couldn't offend anyone by singling anyone out. We didn't have to because they all understand.

We stop at the end of the hall in front of the minister. Paige turns to me and clasps both my hands. Her eyes overflow with happy tears. I've never seen such a magnificent smile blasting light and joy out of her face.

This is all mine. I'm the one who gets to see her happy, sad, furious, devastated, annoyed, half-asleep, and groaning in pain when she comes home from the dentist. All those shades of her are mine to treasure. That's the woman I'm marrying today.

The minister gives his speech about what marriage means—like she and I and everyone else in this room don't already know. I already know about the hard times, the ghosts of the past, the horror stories, the little friction points that make each of us unique.

I want it all. I want the bad stuff as well as the good stuff. I especially want the bad stuff. Those are the times when I really love her. Loving her through the good times is too easy. I want to prove myself by being there for the hard shit.

I want to help her through it. I want to be the one who stood by her when the rest of the world went to trash and beat her down, I want to be the one who saw her at her worst and still loved her for it. That's what marriage is to me.

I want to be the one who shares the darkest secrets of her heart—the stuff she's never had the courage to tell anyone else—because I already am. I'm the one she comes to when she's unsure of herself and thinks she completely screwed everything up.

I'm the one she tells the worst fears and injuries of her past. I'm the one she falls asleep with at night and lets see her messy and puffy-eyed every morning.

Those are the moments I cherish. Those moments are the real reward—not the good times. Those are the moments I'm marrying her for.

I would marry her right now even if I knew we would never have any good times. I would marry her if I knew the rest of our lives would be utter shit. I would marry her just for that—so I could go through it with her.

It won't be. Life is too damn good. She makes everything better just by being here, holding my hands, and smiling up at me while she chokes out her vows.

She promises to love, honor, and cherish me in sickness and in health, for richer or poorer, for better or for worse, until death do we part. Hell yes. I'm there. Let's go. Bring it on. Bring on all of it.

She slips the ring onto my finger and I slip mine onto hers. It looks perfect next to her engagement band. That moron Trent only gave her the plain gold wedding band and nothing else. Did he even propose to her?

He's the loser in this whole equation. I hope he's happy rotting away down there in North Carolina. Now I'm the one discovering what could have been his greatest treasure—the treasure he threw away for no reason at all.

Now she's mine. I scoop her up in my arms, spin her around, and kiss her in front of the whole crowd. She laughs as her long train gets wound around my legs so I can't move.

The crowd erupts in cheers and laughter. Our friends throw rice over me and Paige. We're married. It's done.

My friends from the club have to come forward to unwind her train so I can move without falling flat on my face. That would make this a wedding no one would ever forget.

Paige and I clasp hands and move off into the crowd to greet, hug, and shake hands with everyone who wants to congratulate us.

Now we can all enjoy ourselves and turn this into the happiest, fanciest, most joyful gala The Billionaires' Club has ever had. None of us will ever forget it—especially not me. Today will go down in history as the greatest day of my life.

<u>End of Book 8.</u>

Keep Reading

The Billionaires' Club Series: Book 9: Falsely Accused

Diego Espinosa doesn't think anything can get any worse than when he walks into his business partner's office and finds the man stabbed to death and bleeding on the ground. Diego is about to find out that things can always get worse when the NYPD accuses him of killing his friend right inside their own office building.

Detective Jocelyn Hitchcock is the last person Diego wants to see showing up at his place of business asking a lot of uncomfortable questions about his affairs. She's his worst enemy, but he's going to find out that Jocelyn isn't what she appears. She's going to prove herself to be his staunchest, most loyal, most courageous ally—the only person who can save him from a fate worse than death.

The investigation spirals into something much bigger that will drag The Billionaires' Club into a scandal from which it might never recover. Diego and Jocelyn get caught in the middle with no one but each other to save them from catastrophe.

You can find it at your favorite book retailer.

Get All of AE Moran's Free Books

S ign Up Once—Get all A.E. Moran's free books including brand new releases

Holden Seager is hot, magnetic, and filthy, stinking, obscenely rich. He commands a room the minute he walks in the door. So what happens when meets another shark as powerful, as charismatic, and as successful as he is—not to mention ten years younger? When these two meet across the negotiating table, one of them will walk away the undisputed winner. The other will walk away with nothing.

Or so it seems.

Unless they're best friends.

When the business deal of a lifetime falls flat on its face and neither of these titans knows how to bring it back to life, this might be the opportunity Dayna Turner has been waiting for.

There's just one problem. She works as an assistant to one of these powerful men....and she's in love with the other. It's a recipe for disaster and heartbreak—unless Dayna can pull off an even bigger coup that will leave them all richer, happier, and more closely connected than ever. The alternative is the destruction of everything all three of them have worked so hard to build.

Sign up at www.authoraemoran.com to read it for free.

About AE Moran

A.E Moran is the contemporary romance pen name for Theo Mann.

I write 70 books per year—and yes, before you ask, all these books are my original creative work. Nothing written under my name is AI-generated or ghostwritten because I write better than AI and any ghostwriter out there.

People don't read fiction for entertainment or to escape from reality. People read fiction to see their humanity reflected in another person's character and story.

This is my promise to you. When you read my books, you'll see your own humanity reflected in the characters and stories. I take this commitment to my readers very seriously. My books are an intimate form of communication between us. I would never disrespect my readers by turning that over to a machine or another writer. This is my bond between me and you as my reader.

I write 20,000 words per day as my daily work output. If anyone with a public platform would like to challenge me to prove this in a controlled environment, feel free to contact me on this website's contact page.

I worked as a professional ghostwriter for fifteen years. Now I'm going for the Guinness World Record by writing 700 books over the next ten years and 1400 books over the next twenty years, all originally written by me. See my website for the full book list.

I'm also the author of *Proof for the Existence of God* and the *Crimes Against Fiction* blog. You can find all my nonfiction work at www.crimes-against-fiction.com.

If you have a story idea, or if you would like me to explore a series in more depth, or if you'd like me to explore a character by writing a spinoff series about that character or world, leave me a message on my website's contact page. I answer all reader emails, so ask me anything, tell me what you liked and didn't like, and let me know where you'd like your favorite series to go. I would love to hear your ideas and find out what you'd like to read next.

You can find out more at www.theomann.com or at www.authoraemoran.com.

Also by AE Moran (so far)